The messenger du[...] quet of white roses in blue tissue onto the stage, right at the club owner's feet, and then she waved the receipt in front of Schirra's nose.

"All right, all right! If it makes you get out of here, I'll sign. But I don't have a goddamn pencil," he said gruffly.

"Anything to oblige," she answered sarcastically, reaching into her worn bag. But that was no pencil in her hand. She had pulled out a small derringer. And now she was using it to shoot Carl Schirra in the face. Twice.

The audience—what there was of it—went wild with panic. Everyone was screaming . . . diving for safety beneath the tables . . . crying.

Didi lay on the floor. She had bruised the heels of her palms while diving for cover. Everything was quiet now . . . everyone was still.

Then Didi heard a rasping sound. At first she thought Carl Schirra was still alive.

But then she saw the sound was coming from Molson. The big gray cat was scratching his back on one of the dead man's shoes.

Dr. Nightingale Meets Puss in Boots

A DEIRDRE QUINN
NIGHTINGALE
MYSTERY

Lydia Adamson

A SIGNET BOOK

SIGNET
Published by the Penguin Group
Penguin Books USA Inc., 375 Hudson Street,
New York, New York 10014, U.S.A.
Penguin Books Ltd, 27 Wrights Lane,
London W8 5TZ, England
Penguin Books Australia Ltd, Ringwood,
Victoria, Australia
Penguin Books Canada Ltd, 10 Alcorn Avenue,
Toronto, Ontario, Canada M4V 3B2
Penguin Books (N.Z.) Ltd, 182–190 Wairau Road,
Auckland 10, New Zealand

Penguin Books Ltd, Registered Offices:
Harmondsworth, Middlesex, England

First published by Signet, an imprint of Dutton Signet,
a division of Penguin Books USA Inc.

First Printing, August, 1997
10 9 8 7 6 5 4 3 2 1

Chapter 1

The taxi was right on time. Eight a.m. exactly. Deirdre Quinn Nightingale, D.V.M., looked through the living room curtain and rolled her eyes heavenward. Along with the four family retainers that she referred to as her elves—who worked for her in return for their room and board—she was headed for a week's vacation in New York City.

The cab would take them to the train station in Poughkeepsie, where they would board the 8:45 for Grand Central Station. Didi had been hoping against hope that something might delay the arrival of the taxi. But it was no good. The driver was opening the trunk now, and her four traveling companions were loading it up with their luggage. The young vet sighed deeply, grabbed her little valise, and went out to join the party.

On the train, the group chattered excitedly about the trip—except for Didi, that is, who was hardly in a party mood. In fact, she was downright glum. But she had good reason to be glum. This was a forced vacation as far as she was concerned. She hadn't wanted to go anywhere at all, and she definitely had no desire to spend a week in Manhattan in the August heat in the company of her elves.

The circumstances that brought this little jaunt into being had been decidedly strange. One week earlier, the United Villages Fair had taken place. It was a two-day event, just outside Hillsbrook, that tried to mimic the massive week-long bacchanal called the Dutchess County Fair, which always occurred around Labor Day.

Didi had served as judge in several of the contests, such as Best Calf and Best Working Dog. All the elves had been in attendance as well.

Mrs. Tunney, Didi's housekeeper, had been one of the judges in the pie baking contest. Didi found this inexplicable, since Mrs. Tunney herself never baked pies. Charlie Gravis,

Didi's geriatric veterinary assistant, had helped out at one of the "pitch and toss" booths. Trent Tucker, the so-called handyman, had hired on as a garbage removal man.

And Abigail, as usual, had just wandered about.

On the second and last day of the fair there was the traditional talent contest. A portable stage was set up and a prize announced. The stage and mike were "open"—anyone could walk up and perform. And they did. There were jugglers, dancers, psychics, yodelers, magicians. There were local rock bands, violinists, and a woman who played "Unforgettable" on old wooden bird cages.

There was even a dog trainer with five Afghan hounds that leaped over one another and then through burning hoops.

And then, to everyone's astonishment, up walked Abigail.

Now, people in Hillsbrook knew that Abigail was one of Dr. Nightingale's elves. They also knew that this thin, very fair and ethereal-looking young woman of twenty-four years was, as someone had once described her, three bales short of a full hayloft.

They knew some other things about Abigail:

She was vaguely related to either Trent Tucker or Mrs. Tunney; while she rarely spoke, she did sing in the church choir; and from time to time she burst out of her shell and into some very outrageous behavior.

But what she did when she walked up on the stage was not outrageous at all.

Abigail simply began to sing—a cappella. She sang three songs that Joan Baez had sung in her early days: "Black Is the Color," "Railroad Bill," and "Blue, You Good Dog You."

Abigail had mesmerized the crowd. And one of the enchanted listeners was a visiting Manhattanite named Carl Schirra, who owned one of those country-western bars—Boots—in the section of New York City known as Chelsea.

Schirra said that folk singers were making a big comeback—that Abigail was a budding star—that he was going to book her into Boots for a week—that he'd pay all hotel expenses for her and her family in New York City (not a fancy hotel, mind you, but a clean one)—that she had to make up her mind now—that this was the chance of a lifetime.

Abigail accepted the offer and announced the news to her "family"—Charlie, Trent, and

Mrs. Tunney. The elves jumped at the invitation, but before the day was out they were begging Didi to accompany them. Not least of all because they were frightened of the Big Bad Apple and Didi was wise to the ways of the city. She had spent several years in vet school in Philadelphia, and that was practically the same thing as being born a city girl, wasn't it?

Didi bent to the pressure. But there was another factor contributing to her decision to make the trip. One of Didi's vet school classmates, Ilona Baer, had opened what had become a very successful small animal practice in the city. Ilona had been asking Didi to visit for years. Didi had postponed the visit time and again. Now she decided that she might as well stun two birds with one stone. Ilona was ecstatic when Didi telephoned to say that she would spend the week with her while the elves stayed at the hotel.

Didi did have a professional reason for visiting Ilona. A week or so with one of the premier young veterinarians in New York City would give her some intensive hands-on experience with diseases of and surgery on cats. Didi was quite happy with her large animal practice in Hillsbrook, but she had always been fascinated with felines and wanted to know more about them.

And there was another enticement. Ilona had developed a passion for cold climes and was always going off on adventures at the North or South Pole, where she studied ecological niches. It was really just a hobby, but she had become so knowledgeable that the Central Park Zoo used her as a part-time nutritional consultant for the polar bears, sea lions, and penguins. The thought that her old school chum was dealing with Gus, the now-world-famous neurotic polar bear who had required psychiatric help, was simply delicious.

The quintet, spread out over three rows of seats on the dreary Amtrak car, was an odd mix. The sixtyish Mrs. Tunney was dressed for a summer church wedding, including a flamboyant hat. Charlie Gravis wore the vest to a long-forgotten Sunday best dress suit over a white T-shirt that was two sizes too big for his small frame. Only a year younger than Abigail, Trent Tucker was wearing snug-fitting black jeans and a faded black denim shirt. He had heard that hip people in Manhattan always wore black. Abigail, the budding heir to Joan Baez's throne, wore her usual shapeless long blue dress. Blue was her favorite color, and she seemed to have a homemade frock in every shade of that color.

As for Didi, she was dressed just as she might be dressed to go out on rounds—denims, washed-out sweatshirt, and rain sneakers. Her only concession to the occasion was the addition of tiny black pearl earrings.

Since Didi was wiry in build and her black hair was cut short, it was entirely possible that someone viewing the entourage would think that here was a set of grandparents taking their three just-out-of-college grandchildren to New York as a graduation present.

Ten minutes outside New York City, the train slowed and then came to a stop. The air-conditioning and the car lights went out. Even though it was still morning, the atmosphere in the car very quickly became stifling.

"I knew we should have taken an earlier train," Mrs. Tunney whined.

"What's our rush?" Charlie replied. "We don't have to be at that nightclub till six in the evening. "Abigail doesn't start singing till seven."

"What about Miss Quinn? What about all her appointments?" Mrs. Tunney kept on.

Didi didn't respond. She had told Mrs. Tunney half a dozen times that she had no appointments at all—that she would spend the whole day with them—and she would leave for her friend Ilona's place after Abigail's debut.

In fact, the only thing that wasn't planned was whether to leave after Abigail's first or second performance. She was scheduled to perform two sets, one at seven and one at nine. Another singer was to perform at eight and again at ten. And then the headliner for the night, a zydeco band, was to go on at eleven.

"We won't be here long," Charlie said reassuringly, staring out the window to assess the situation. He spoke with supreme authority, as if he were an old hand at such things, a veteran railroad man.

The train sat immobile for one hour and nineteen minutes. It pulled into Grand Central Station two hours late.

The hotel that Carl Schirra selected for them was called the Kenmare. It was only three blocks away from the station and was one of those new "all suite" places that provide multi-room accommodations at reasonable prices, and virtually no services. It had been converted from a welfare hotel.

They took their own bags up to the third floor and entered a rather nice complex of rooms: a large living room, two small bedrooms, a tiny kitchen, and a bathroom. The suite was heavily air-conditioned, actually cold.

Everyone washed up and changed. They all seemed happy that, the stalled train aside, there had been no major disasters. They rested for an hour, then walked to 34th Street and ate hugely at a fast-food Italian place called Sbarro's. Their next stop was Macy's.

Sometime during their spree at the world's largest store they lost both Abigail and Charlie Gravis. It wasn't until 3:20 P.M. that store security located Abigail, who was standing on the corner of 35th and 7th Avenue, across the street from the store. At 3:45 they found Charlie fast asleep in a lounger in the furniture department.

Worse than that, Trent Tucker had spent his entire cash reserve on a pair of Elvis-type boots.

"It could have been worse," Didi reminded her troops, and herself, after they landed back in the hotel with all the packages and all the bodies.

The problem was that it was now almost five and Schirra had told them to be at Boots by six. "We have fifteen minutes to dress," Didi announced.

Chaos ensued, but the task got done. They were ready for dear Abigail's leap from obscurity to America's most beloved warbler.

A cab transported them to 10th Avenue and 22nd Street. "I love this city!" Trent Tucker declared to the Nigerian driver as he exited. It was Didi who paid the fare.

As they approached Boots, Mrs. Tunney stopped in her tracks. She had halted so suddenly that she tripped up Abigail. Charlie helped the folk singer regain her feet. He barked at the old housekeeper, "What's the matter with you, woman?"

Now pale, she answered, "I just had the terrible feeling that something is going to go wrong up in Hillsbrook."

"Stop worrying. Everything is covered," Didi said in her professional soother's manner. And indeed, everything was. Didi's best friend, Rose Vigdor, had volunteered to look after the yard dogs, the hogs, and the horse. As for the Nightingale veterinary practice, two local vets were covering that.

The entourage proceeded.

"Where's Abigail's name at?" Trent Tucker demanded when they reached the front door of the club.

There was no marquee, no poster or announcement of anyone except the headlining zydeco band, the Bayou Blasters. And even the flyer announcing them had been done on the cheap: a plain white piece of photocopy paper with the words TONIGHT! THE BAYOU BLASTERS lettered in red Magic Marker and thumbtacked to a board next to the entrance.

Once the group was inside the club, Didi realized that Boots was not what she'd expected. It wasn't even close to what she'd expected. There was a long, narrow bar up front. Past that the space grew wide enough to accommodate about fifteen small tables with four chairs placed around each. A raised wooden stage was nestled along the back wall so that bar patrons as well as the customers at the table could see and hear the show.

On the stage was a standing microphone, a full set of drums, and some sound equipment. The walls were covered with reproductions of

Wild West–era Wanted posters, particularly variations of the William Bonney—alias Billy the Kid—posters.

"Are you the people from Hillsbrook?" asked the petite lady bartender.

"Four from Hillsbrook, one from the moon," quipped Charlie Gravis, pointing to Trent Tucker, who had obviously fallen instantaneously in love with the young woman.

"I'm Arden," she said. She came out and led the contingent to a table, pulling up two extra chairs.

Carl Schirra then popped up out of nowhere and greeted them all extravagantly—as if Abigail were Streisand and the others her retinue.

Arden left and came back with five bottles of Sierra Nevada Pale Ale, five tall glasses, and two big bowls of popcorn. She poured the ale for them under Mrs. Tunney's baleful gaze.

Suddenly, Mrs. Tunney screamed.

A large gray Persian cat had appeared from nowhere, jumped up, and was now draped across her lap. The cat's long tail was swishing happily.

Arden came to the rescue of the startled Mrs. Tunney. She pulled the cat off the beleaguered housekeeper and held him up admiringly. "It's just his way of being friendly. This is Molson. He lives here. He's been a bit under the weather, but he seems to be fine now." Then she let Molson down and the big cat wandered off.

Didi watched him move. Mrs. Tunney apologized for her fright. "It's not that I don't like cats," she explained. "It's just that it was so sudden, and he's so . . . big."

"Yes," Charlie Gravis said, "he sure is big. I like big cats and little women."

Trent Tucker laughed. Mrs. Tunney gave Charlie a look informing him she didn't think his comment was funny.

Schirra, who was a darkly handsome middle-aged man with a bushy mustache and friendly eyes, leaned over and kissed Abigail's cheek. "You're on in thirty-five minutes. I'll intro you."

Then he was gone. Didi looked around the place. It was empty; not one other patron had come in. Oh well, she thought, there was still time for an audience to gather.

For a moment, sitting there with her elves, Dr. Nightingale felt very good—a kind of warm déjà vu had come upon her. It was as if she were back in school in Philadelphia and she and her chums had gone to a funky bar in South Philly to relax and celebrate after exams.

That feeling evaporated when a tipsy middle-aged man entered the room and worked his way back to a table. He looked quite lost.

Then another table was occupied by two women wearing flamboyant print summer dresses and drinking Bloody Marys. They looked like schoolteachers from the Midwest on a binge.

The audience was completed when a well-dressed young man came in, sat at a front table, and immediately began working on the *New York Times* crossword puzzle.

Well, Didi thought, it probably gets crowded later on. It probably will be packed for Abigail's second set, at nine. And it will probably be a very young crowd—with nary a single middle-aged lush.

Trent Tucker ordered five more ales even though neither Mrs. Tunney nor Abigail nor Didi had touched hers. "Who's paying for this?" Charlie demanded.

"Who cares?" Trent retorted, shrugging his shoulders.

Didi began to watch Abigail for signs of anxiety or anticipation. There seemed to be none.

Abigail just sat quietly, her eyes on a nearby Wanted poster. The outfit she had chosen to perform in was one of Didi's mother's old dresses, loose white cotton with maroon stitching at the sleeves and neck, along with white flat-heeled sandals.

Mr. Schirra reappeared. This time he was wearing a blue blazer with a red bow tie. He walked to the wall beside the stage and flicked a switch. The bar lights dimmed, and the stage lights went on.

He climbed the stage and fiddled with the mike—using the standard *one two three* testing script—until he got it adjusted.

"Ladies and gentlemen, welcome to Boots. It is not often that a club owner like myself has the good luck of discovering an awesome new talent. I am not a man who trades in superlatives, so when I say awesome I mean—"

"Hey!"

The shout had come from the bar area, bringing Schirra's introduction to a halt. The audience and Schirra all looked back at what was apparently a bike messenger, a chunky young blond woman sporting a helmet and tight-fitting Lycra cycling pants. Arden, the pretty bartender, tried to silence the girl, but to no avail.

"Where do you want these?" the messenger yelled to Schirra and held up a bouquet of cut flowers. "And I need a signature," she added testily.

"What the hell is the matter with you?" Schirra shouted back angrily. "Can't you see there's a performance going on here? You deliver flowers *after* a performance, you nitwit." He then glared down at the Hillsbrook table, as if to imply they had to have been responsible for the transgression.

The messenger shrugged and began walking boldly toward the stage. She dumped the bedraggled bouquet of white roses wrapped in blue tissue onto the stage, right at the club owner's feet, and then she waved the receipt in front of the steaming Schirra's nose.

"All right, all right! If it'll make you get out of here, I'll sign. But I don't have a goddamn pencil," he said gruffly.

"Anything to oblige," she answered sarcastically, reaching into her worn bag.

But that was no pencil in her hand. She had pulled out a small derringer. And now she was using it to shoot Carl Schirra in the face. Twice.

The girl ran lightly out of the club as the dying man fell off the stage and onto the lap of the young man with the newspaper, splattering him and his crossword with blood.

The audience—what there was of it—went wild with panic. Everyone screaming—diving for safety beneath the tables—crying.

Schirra had managed to entwine one of the many long cords on the stage around his leg as he fell. The microphone wobbled a few times and hit the wooden floor with the most horrible scream of all.

Didi lay on the floor. She had bruised the heels of her palms while diving for cover. Everything was quiet now. Everything and everyone was still.

Then Didi heard a rasping sound. At first she thought Carl Schirra was still alive. But then she saw that the sound was coming from Molson. The big gray cat was scratching his back on one of the dead man's shoes.

Chapter 2

Dr. Nightingale didn't say a word when the fight erupted among her elves. After all, four hours after the murder they were still being detained in Boots. Everyone's nerves were on edge.

The body had been removed. But the lab technicians were still there, along with a photographer, two detectives, and an NYPD artist. The latter had come in from the precinct to do a sketch of the murderess based on recollections of the eyewitnesses.

The fight, or rather the argument, erupted when Abigail, who hadn't said a word since the murder, suddenly announced: "I don't want to sing here. I want to go home."

Trent Tucker burst out laughing at her comment. Mrs. Tunney told him to shut his mouth.

Charlie Gravis defended the boy and soon everyone was yelling at everyone.

One of the detectives a few tables over, the one named Phil Slater, raised his hands, cocked his head, and stared hard at Didi. She knew he was asking her to exert some control over her troops. You are a fool, Detective, she thought. I can't control them in Hillsbrook after a meal . . . so how can I control them in Manhattan after a murder?

That was what she was thinking. But she made an accommodating motion to the police officer to indicate that she would try to quiet her companions.

Then Didi herself leaped into the fray. "Mrs. Tunney, what's to be done!" she cried out pathetically, as if she needed help and only the older woman could supply it.

The ploy worked. Mrs. Tunney shut up. So did the others. The boss needed help. Dr. Nightingale continued, "Are you all going to stay on a few days?"

"Abigail wants to go back now. And that's what we're going to do," Mrs. Tunney said. "Tonight!"

"The next train is midmorning," Didi noted.

"If the hotel is paid up," Trent Tucker said,

"why not stay on? We haven't even seen the city yet."

Mrs. Tunney ignored him. She said, "I knew there was going to be trouble the minute that big, ugly old cat jumped up on me. Where is he now?"

"On the bar, near the register," Charlie said. They all turned and stared at the dozing cat.

"I want to go home," Abigail repeated in a low voice. Everyone at the table started getting nervous. Abigail had already gone beyond her usual speaking portion. And she rarely made these kind of "I want" statements twice. The murder had been quite enough. Abigail spinning out of control would have been just too much to bear.

"We're going home tomorrow morning bright and early," Charlie Gravis announced with authority and finality, patting Abigail reassuringly on the arm while glaring at Trent Tucker to let him know that no one was staying in the Big Apple—except the boss, if she wanted to.

The argument over and settled, there was silence. Trent began to play morosely with the beer bottles. From time to time he looked up, trying to catch sight of the lady bartender. But he could catch only a part of her profile. She was busy at a far table, consulting with the police artist, who was working on a large pad.

Didi went to the ladies' room and poured water over the heels of her palms, which had been bruised when she dived for cover.

When she came out, she wandered over to the bar and tried to start a conversation with Molson. The big cat was not interested. She wondered how cats in general react, psychologically, to brutal murders of humans.

Dr. Nightingale turned around and leaned against the bar. The shock of the murder had passed. In fact, she felt oddly disconnected from it—as if it had happened on a television show, rather than right there in front of her. The dead man, Carl Schirra, was only a name and a face.

She rested her elbows on the bar, like an outlaw in a cowboy movie.

There were so many strange things to deal with. For one, it had turned out, according to the detectives, that the blond murderess in the bike messenger outfit had no bike. For another, why would such a miserable chain of events happen to poor innocent Abigail?

That, of course, was a philosophical question. Didi spun back toward the cat and asked, "And why *did* you jump up on Mrs. Tunney's lap?" The cat did not answer, but he did at last make eye contact with Didi.

I am getting foolish, she thought; I need some sleep.

She gazed out once again at the tableau. Her elves seemed truly to have quieted down. They looked now like exhausted strangers in a strange land. And the NYPD seemed to be wrapping things up.

The most curious thing of all, she mused, was how she had misread the audience for Abigail's aborted debut. The middle-aged "lush" turned out to be a distinguished physician named Ron Besser. The two women she had thought were midwestern schoolteachers on vacation were actually Janice and Pat Mazzini, sisters from Brooklyn who worked at the United Nations. And the strange young man with the crossword puzzle was Darryl Yates, who owned a small trucking company.

Didi realized that her usually reliable antennae about people and their occupations and their geographic origins had been dysfunctional all evening.

"So you're a vet!"

She turned. One of the detectives was now standing right next to her. She hadn't even heard him approach. It was the younger one, Louie Follette. He was wiping his brow and neck with a folded white handkerchief, then refolding and wiping again. His shirt was dark from sweat.

"Yes, I am," Didi said.

"From Hillsbrook, right?"

"Right."

"That's in Dutchess County."

"Right."

"Pretty town. I drove through it once."

"Yes, it is," she agreed.

If she had a dime for every person she met who told her he or she had been through Hillsbrook once or twice and thought it pretty—well, she would now have a mansion outside of Hillsbrook, overlooking the Hudson.

The detective leaned over the bar to the service side, retrieved some ice cubes, and rubbed them along his neck until they were spent, watery slivers.

"I wanted to be a vet when I was a kid," he confided.

"Is that right?"

And if Didi had a dime for every person

who'd told her that he or she dreamed of becoming a veterinarian at one point in life—she would have already been retired from the practice of veterinary medicine and would be breeding horses somewhere in Spain or California.

"Did you ever treat an elephant?" he asked.

"Yes. Several."

"Damn!" exclaimed Detective Follette in awe.

Didi's thoughts turned to Allie Voegler. This was the first time they had been apart since they had become lovers. She should have called him already and told him what happened. But, being a cop, he wouldn't have said a word about the murder except to nail down the essentials. And being a jealous lover, he would have given her one of those bitter I told you so's. Allie didn't like her elves. And, quite frankly, they didn't like him. Mrs. Tunney was continually looking for a romantic replacement for Voegler. In fact, only two days before the trip to Manhattan, Didi had overheard Mrs. Tunney say to Charlie Gravis, "Her mother must be turning over in her grave. The child can do so much better."

"What about an eagle? Did you ever treat an eagle?" the detective asked.

"Golden or Bald or Monkey?" Didi shot back.

That stumped her questioner. She excused herself and headed for the table where the artist was reconstructing the face of the young bike messenger without a bike.

Didi stood in front of the building, by the curb, and stared up in wonderment. It was the largest apartment house she had ever seen, dwarfing even the giants that had been erected in center city Philadelphia during her tenure at vet school there.

To her left was First Avenue, and even though it was one o'clock in the morning, the big trucks were there, rumbling uptown, coming from somewhere and obviously heading somewhere.

To her right was the East River, and just a bit downtown was the heliport pad with the dragonflies buzzing in and out twenty-four hours a day.

Didi felt silly staring up like a yokel, but she couldn't help it. The massive structure seemed to capture one's eyes and pull them, like a beautiful dress. The problem was, this structure wasn't beautiful. It was ugly, overpoweringly ugly.

Then she walked inside and told the doorman that she was there to see Dr. Ilona Baer. The doorman, a young Hispanic resplendent in a tan uniform with the name of the building emblazoned over his breast, was patently suspicious.

"The entrance to her office is on the other side of the building, miss—on the ground floor. But it's closed now."

Didi didn't respond.

"If you have an emergency, go to the dog and cat hospital on York and 63rd. They're open all night."

"Please let her know she has a visitor."

"It's one o'clock in the morning," the doorman noted.

"Yes, I'm aware of the time. Just call her and tell her that Nightingale is here."

So the doorman rang Ilona Baer and the visit was approved. Didi took the high-speed elevator to the 46th floor. The door opened.

"Hello, Nightingale."

"Hello, Baer."

And the two old friends were reunited—the

first time they had seen each other since vet school graduation. No wonder they immediately called each other now what they had called each other in school.

Ilona led Didi into the apartment by the hand. It was a dazzling place—huge, sprawling—surrounded on two sides by windows that looked north and east.

And Ilona herself was now dazzling. She wore a very expensive designer bathrobe. She wore her once long black hair in a stylish short cut. And she had lost a great deal of weight. Didi could not help noticing how Ilona talked in a kind of clipped, precise manner, like a Valley Girl who had gone to Oxford for a course in speed reading.

"First off, Nightingale," she said, pushing Didi down on a sectional and bringing her a massive bowl of fresh fruit, cheese, utensils, napkins, and crackers, "where the hell have you been? You were supposed to get here about ten. So the clock keeps ticking, and I'm thinking something bad happened or something so good it won't be believed. Either you got hit by a truck or that girl—what's her name—sang so beautifully that you had to stay late to start signing recording contracts for her."

"It was something bad, Baer," Didi said, keeping the old form of address, which originally had been a defense against male professors using the term "Miss" with a vengeance.

Then Didi described the murder of Carl Schirra.

"Do the police know why the girl shot him?"

"They seem to know nothing."

"Well, everyone knows that night club owners in New York are into strange things. Maybe it was a mob hit."

"The girl didn't look like a mobster," Didi said.

"Appearances are deceptive," Ilona replied. Then she held her hand up suddenly. "I remember something!" she exclaimed.

"What?"

"That name."

"Schirra?"

"Yes. What was his first name?"

"Carl."

"And the name of the club?"

"Boots."

"Where is it?"

"On Tenth Avenue. I think the neighborhood is called Chelsea."

Then Ilona shook her head sadly. "No. I lost it. I mean I seemed to have heard that name before. Somewhere . . . a while ago. But I can't nail it down."

"You mean a client?"

"No. Just someone mentioning that name to me, maybe just in passing. Well, it'll come to me."

And then they settled back and talked about their old friends and teachers. Then their new friends. And their lovers, past and present. And their enemies.

Ilona even brought out a slide projector and at three in the morning showed slides of herself in her new hobby—arctic and antarctic exploration. In fact, she explained happily, she had become so caught up in it that the New York Zoological Society had made her a nutritional consultant for the polar bears, sea lions, and penguins.

Didi found all this most peculiar. Why would a young vet who had quickly built up a successful practice embark on strange hobbies that took her thousands of miles from that practice? But Ilona Baer was always a bit quirky, a bit wild.

The air conditioner kept on purring. The fruit bowl seemed never to diminish. And then there was wine and coffee.

"My God!" Ilona said. "It's almost five o'clock in the morning and you still haven't said a word about cows."

Didi grimaced.

"Come on, Nightingale!"

Didi laughed. Once, in that bar in South Philly the vet students used to frequent after particularly ugly exams, they had spent hours making up lewd ditties about cows. "There once was a cow from Peoria . . ."

Five in the morning. The time finally registered on Didi. She realized there was no way she could make it to the train station in a few hours to see her elves off. But so what? They knew how to get home.

Didi cut herself a small wedge of cheese, placed it on a tiny gourmet cracker, and stared past Ilona—out the window, catching a glimpse of the lighted spires of the Triboro Bridge in the distance. She closed her eyes for a moment, longing for sleep.

Then she opened them brightly, took a bite,

crunched, swallowed, and said, "You want to hear about cows, Baer? Well, you came to the right place. I'm just a little old country vet. And the one thing I do know is cows. I'm gonna tell you about dairy cows until you scream for mercy."

Twenty minutes into the train ride back to Hillsbrook, Mrs. Tunney got "the shivers."

This was a low-grade condition that always beset her when bad things happened. Her stomach would turn sour. Her back would ache. And her legs would start to tremble ever so slightly.

She did what she always did when the shivers came on her—she closed her eyes, breathed in and out slowly (much as Dr. Nightingale did during her early morning yoga), and wiggled her toes constantly.

Poor Mr. Schirra! That nice man—getting killed that way. Oh, Mrs. Tunney had seen a lot in her life. Terrible things had happened in Hillsbrook. But never a pretty young lady just walking up to a man with a bouquet of flowers and shooting him to death without mercy.

The shivers were subsiding. She recited the 23rd Psalm to herself, then opened her eyes and surveyed her charges. And charges were exactly what they were. For even though they were all adults, they were still her responsibility—all of them. This had been a terrible experience, and it was her job to get them all through it.

Abigail was sitting quietly. She seemed peaceful enough. She was even smiling a bit and may well have been thinking of something nice.

The only thing about Abigail's demeanor right then that troubled Mrs. Tunney was that it was obvious the young woman had not given her long golden hair a good brushing before checking out of the hotel. She was a bit disheveled. And . . . Abigail did have her hands folded strangely on her lap—as though she were a very young girl again at school.

Trent Tucker was another matter altogether. He was alternately staring daggers at her or sullenly out the train window. Mrs. Tunney knew he was very angry. She knew how much he had looked forward to the trip. She knew how he craved the excitement of the big city. And she knew he had got himself hypnotized by that pretty young bartender.

Well, she thought, it was probably for the best that we all went back immediately. Trent was always getting into some kind of trouble in Hillsbrook. Imagine the kind of trouble he could get into in New York City. It was enough to make a body shudder.

As for Charlie Gravis . . . he just looked sad. She knew why: Old Charlie had really thought that this was going to be *the* break—the end of his poverty. For years he had been hatching those penny ante schemes, all of them crazy, to make some real money—like secret herbal remedies for ailing livestock or a system for winning the million-dollar lottery. Every one of them had failed. Abigail, he had thought, was finally going to bring home the bacon.

Mrs. Tunney sighed and shook her head. He's past seventy already, she thought, and he still can't accept his lot. Poor fool.

Mrs. Tunney's face suddenly lit up. Heavens! She had forgotten what she had purchased surreptitiously in the terminal before they had boarded the train.

She reached down into her voluminous bag and pulled out the waxed paper bag with the bakery logo on it. She had purchased four jelly donuts. One for each of them.

Two o'clock. Didi couldn't believe it. She sat up abruptly.

Two o'clock when? Morning? No. It had to be afternoon. The light was flooding through the windows.

She remembered where she was.

"Baer!" she called out.

There was no answer. She slipped into her jeans, threw on a faded sweatshirt with cut-down sleeves, and walked quickly into the living room. The powerful air conditioner made the apartment like an icebox. Didi was not used to such a cooling system. During the sleeping hours it had tightened her neck and given her a slight headache. Her nose was a bit stuffed also.

There was a note on the low coffee table. She rotated her neck as she read it. "Come down to the office as soon as you're up. Coffee on stove. Three muffins in bag on counter. Jump in, Nightingale!"

Didi drank two cups of black coffee and then ate half a cinnamon apple muffin. Then she rushed out—down the elevator, out of the building, into the heat, around the corner, and into Ilona Baer's veterinary establishment.

The moment she opened the door a middle-aged receptionist behind a beautiful desk said, "Dr. Nightingale, I presume. She's waiting for you." She then pointed to the door of one of the examining rooms.

Didi nodded and looked around. This was the waiting room, obviously. Only one patient was waiting: a Brittany spaniel, very calm, being lectured to quietly by a nervous owner.

Didi knocked and walked into the examining room. She was almost bowled over by what she saw: a glistening high-tech space with aluminum examining tables, gleaming washbasins, track lighting, a sloping tile floor with drains, elaborate sterilizing equipment, portable X-ray machines. And presiding over it all was Baer in a sparkling starched white smock.

Oh, yes, there were clients in the room, too—a Mrs. Knight, along with her Siamese cat, Winsome, who was on the examination table.

And there was an impeccably clad, somewhat dour veterinary assistant, a young man named Harky, who was fiddling with the computer.

After all the introductions were made, Didi whispered to Ilona, "I'm sorry about my outfit."

Ilona laughed and whispered back, "You look stunning. Like *Country Life*'s idea of what a young country vet should look like. Who else would wear a cut-down sweatshirt in August?"

Then Ilona scooped the startled Winsome off the table and held her out to be admired. "What do you think, Nightingale? How does she look?"

"Damn healthy," Didi replied, laughing, but a bit uncomfortable in front of Mrs. Knight.

Ilone put the cat down. "Pica," she said to Didi.

"Pica?"

"That's it. Depraved appetite. She was sucking wool and eating all kinds of cloth. But we fixed the little devil up with some juicy phosphorus supplements and a few other goodies."

Ilona turned to Mrs. Knight. "Just discontinue the supplements now. If it starts again, start the medication again. If there are any other problems, just call me. Remember, Mrs. Knight, Pica is common in Siamese and

Siamese crosses. Some people think it's genetic."

Then the assistant, Harky, gave Winsome a treat and ushered the happy duo out.

"You have another patient," Didi said.

"You mean Sir Galahad, the Brittany. Did you ever notice that spaniels and their keepers tend to be hypochondriacal?"

"No," Didi admitted.

"And they also—"

Ilona stopped suddenly, midsentence. She looked pained and confused.

"What's the matter?"

"I just remembered something. Oh, yes! It just came to me."

She turned and walked through a doorway at the rear of the examining room and into a spacious private office. Didi stayed where she was, but she peered in. The walls were covered with photos and mementos of Ilona's new passion, frigid flora and fauna.

Didi watched her friend dial a number and then speak in an excited voice. She thought she heard the name Schirra.

Ilona began to gesture wildly that Didi should come into the office. Didi walked in. Ilona pointed to a huge leather chair. Didi sat down. The air conditioner in the office was even more powerful than the one in the apartment. It was positively frigid.

Ilona hung up the phone almost triumphantly. "Do you know who that was?" she asked.

"No."

"Krista Michaels."

"Who's that?"

"Oh, this wonderful looney-tunes rich lady. I take care of her beasts—all of them. She has a reformed alley cat named Sweet William, a Chow bitch named Pinky, and, believe it or not, a very large tortoise named Gruesome. Krista always thinks Gruesome is sick. 'Why is he so sluggish?' she always asks me. 'Could you give Gruesome something to pep him up?' Oh, Krista is something else. But I didn't call her about the tortoise. I suddenly remembered where I had heard the name Carl Schirra before. Krista told me about him a few years ago. She had been going with a man who lived on a houseboat on the Hudson at the 79th Street boat marina, and he also owned a nightclub called Boots. Krista said she heard about the murder. And yes, it was the same man. She hadn't spoken to him for about a year, maybe two. But he was, she said, one of the kindest men she ever went with—and believe me, Krista has gone through a lot of men."

Ilona started to open and close the cabinet doors with a fury. Then she laughed sheepishly. "I was looking for a cigarette. I forgot that I stopped smoking a year ago."

"I never treated a tortoise," Didi said.

"That's O.K. Krista wants to meet you anyway. I told her you were there . . . at the murder scene. She's giving a party tomorrow night. She wants us both there, Nightingale. Are you game?"

"Sure."

"Good. You've never seen anything like Krista Michaels's place. It's amazing. A few pieces of furniture hidden in a triplex greenhouse. Besides . . . it's about time a country bumpkin like yourself, who of course is deep down a very sophisticated lady, met some of the beautiful people." She used the index and forefingers of both hands to mimic the quotation marks around the word "beautiful."

"That was what I went to vet school for," Didi said sarcastically. Her quip hurt Ilona. She pouted, but only for a moment.

"On to Sir Galahad," she said.

They walked back into the examining room.

Rose Vigdor walked out of the big Nightingale house and climbed into her wreck of a car, shouting at her three dogs in the back to behave themselves or else. The dogs kept barking and jumping from front to back—from back to front—and even sideways.

Rose leaned her head wearily on the wheel. What a grotesque series of events. Poor Didi—and Poor Abigail!

Mrs. Tunney had told her the whole story, from beginning to end, with relish.

As to when Didi would return to Hillsbrook, Mrs. Tunney simply didn't know. It could be weeks for all she knew—unless there was a severe veterinary emergency with one of her good clients.

Rose lifted her head and stared at the house. No, Didi wouldn't be away for weeks. She hadn't wanted to go in the first place.

But Rose wanted to talk to her right now. Should she call that vet Didi was staying with in New York? No.

Rose was suddenly ashamed of herself. Never borrow money from a friend—and surely not your best friend. Besides, Didi probably didn't have any cash on hand.

Huck, the Corgi, was now clawing at the glove compartment. He always wanted to get in there. The two shepherds were barking encouragement.

I have to reevaluate my situation, Rose thought. Do I really need the $5,000? She picked up Huck and turned his head so that they were face-to-face. "Do I really need the $5,000?"

The Corgi wriggled out of her grasp and leaped onto the backseat.

Bozo, the young shepherd, leaped into the front seat, crushing Rose against the wheel for a moment. She scratched Bozo's ear with one free hand. He groaned and released the pressure, sitting up, panting.

Rose had, oddly enough, made a key decision last night, one of the hottest nights of the year, about the coming winter. She was going to end her "nature girl" existence in her perpetually unfinished barn with no running water or electricity or heat, except for a primitive wood-burning stove. She was going to call a contractor and have him wire the damn place.

Why, on the hottest night of the year, her thoughts should turn to the misery of enduring another frigid winter was simply too mysterious to understand.

She took a sweet-potato chip from the package on the dash and chewed it thoughtfully. I shall abide by my decision, she thought. I shall raise the $5,000. I will spend the next winter in Hillsbrook in glorious warmth.

That's that!

For a brief moment she cursed herself for going through the small nest egg she had left over after buying the barn and the property and moving upstate from Manhattan. God, where had it all gone?

Then she turned the key in the ignition and the motor started. But she didn't move the shift into drive. Another vehicle had pulled off the road about fifty yards from the house.

It was the Hillsbrook Police Department's only unmarked cruiser. And at the wheel, Rose could see, was that department's only plainclothes detective, Allie Voegler. He looked like a mournful bear hunched over the wheel, his large frame awkward in the driver's seat.

Rose was perplexed. Was he staking out the Nightingale place?

Then a sad smile. Oh, no. Not a stakeout. It was a vigil, she realized. He was waiting for his true love. Rose didn't know whether to laugh or cry. These country men were so strange. Since moving to Hillsbrook from the city, Rose had ascertained that upstate males were just as smart and sophisticated as their downstate counterparts—in every area but one. They seemed to be retarded in affairs of the heart. They were just like little boys.

What the hell was Allie going to do? Show up every day on the road and just pine until his lady love came back?

She pushed the lever into drive and passed his standing vehicle with a wave. The moment she passed his vehicle she forgot him. There was $5,000 on her mind. And there was also the now firm belief that the only way to get that money fast was to sell some of her land. And choice land it was.

"Aretha!" she called out, addressing her old shepherd bitch, who was now reclining on the backseat. "Put it down in our appointment book. Tomorrow or the next day we are paying a visit to our friendly real estate agent. Do you hear me, Aretha?"

Chapter 3

Dr. Nightingale hadn't expected her trip to New York City to include a beautiful people's party. She was unprepared. She needed something to wear. Ilona recommended the Gap. "It has now become chic," she said. So Didi went to a Gap store and purchased a pair of lightweight tan cotton and rayon slacks, a pair of green canvas boating sneakers, and a green polo shirt.

"Exquisite!" pronounced Ilona. And Didi was ready.

They sat around the apartment and chatted. Ilona said: "You have no idea how happy I am you came, Nightingale."

Didi didn't know quite how to respond. She hadn't really come to New York City to see Ilona. She had come with her elves to launch

Abigail's career. The visit to Ilona was merely a—she searched her mind for a nice way to put it—pleasant side trip. Also, Ilona's use of the word "happy" made Didi feel a bit uncomfortable, given the murderous events that had transpired.

"You are going to enjoy the party, Nightingale. I guarantee it."

"It's been so long since I went to a real party, I don't think I know what to do."

"You do nothing. You just do absolutely nothing. The party happens to you."

Didi smiled and ran her right hand along the crease of her new summer slacks. She wondered if Mrs. Tunney would approve of her new outfit. She wondered what Allie Voegler would think of it.

"Did I ever tell you my theory of why domestic cats like fish?"

"No."

"Well, don't you find it curious that they do?"

"Not really," Didi responded, a bit perplexed by the subject. Who cared?

But Ilona was off and running. "For the most part, the cat in the wild doesn't hunt or eat fish. Not the big cats—lions, tigers, leopards. And not the small ones—civet, ocelot, lynx."

"You have a point," Didi agreed.

"My theory is that it was a learned behavior pattern. The common house cat probably became domesticated around mills that ground wheat, corn, and millet. They were enticed to stay in order to control the rodent population where the grain was stored. Do you get it?"

"I'm afraid not."

"Where were the mills built?"

"I don't know."

"Invariably, along swift-running streams to harness the energy to turn the grinding wheels. Water mills. And swift-running streams mean a few dead fish. Carrion. By the water's edge. Mr. Cat comes upon it, takes a bite, likes it. Then learns to hunt the live fish.

"Interesting," Didi noted. She found the subject bizarre. But Ilona always seemed to come up with strange subjects out of the blue.

"And because it was basically a learned behavior, this eating fish, when modern-day feline nutrition experts removed bony and scaly fish from the diets of domestic cats, there were no bad consequences at all. Acquired tastes are irrelevant in the life of a species."

"Sounds logical," Didi said. She had a feeling that if she really probed Baer's theory, she would find enough holes to sink a tanker.

They left five minutes later. The cab dropped them in front of a row of attached houses on upper West End Avenue, sandwiched between two massive old apartment buildings at either end of the block.

Ilona led Didi up the stairs of the brownstone on the left and rang the bell. A man in a white tunic and sporting one gold earring opened the door.

"Pizza?" he inquired, then laughed and waved them in.

"I hope," he said, "you are not uninvited guests, like me."

Didi stopped short a few steps into the room. She looked as if she had been struck dumb.

"Isn't it amazing?" Ilona whispered.

Indeed it was. The entire back wall of the four-story brownstone, from the basement to the roof, had been replaced with greenhouse windows and the floors cut away. The house was filled with plants and trees and flowers—orchids, roses, flowering succulents, and bamboo. Didi had never before seen indoor bamboo stands of such height. They were breathtaking.

The party was already in progress. Ramps along the side walls led up to alcoves on various floors with sofas and chairs—like a theater with parquet boxes.

"Ilona! How nice to see you!"

Didi turned to the quiet but intense voice. A small, sparrowlike woman was standing quietly about five feet away, off to one side, in the shadows. She was wearing a lovely black robe that made her look like an initiate in some kind of Asian meditation cult. Her hair was gray and cropped close to her head. In spite of the hair, her face seemed almost childlike.

"Krista, this is Dr. Deirdre Quinn Nightingale. Didi, Krista Michaels."

Didi held out her hand. The woman grabbed her arm instead, tightly.

"You were there, weren't you?" she asked in a hushed voice.

Didi didn't know what she was talking about. Ilona made her hand into a gun. Didi understood.

"Yes. I was there."

"You saw him die?" Her voice was getting quieter and more tremulous.

"Yes."

"Oh, my God! How horrible it must have been! Did he suffer?"

"I think he died instantly."

"What was he doing when they shot him?"

"It wasn't a they. It was a she—a young blond woman dressed in a bike messenger outfit. At least that's what someone told me it was. Bicyclists don't dress like that where I come from. Anyway, she shot him while he was introducing a new singer. He was on the stage."

"Did she say why? Does anyone know why?" Now her voice was rising.

"No. She brought him a bouquet of roses."

"What a sick world!" Krista Michaels hissed, releasing her grip on Didi's arm. "And what a kind, good man he was!"

She shook her head and walked off. Didi and Ilona moved deeper into the party. The guests were dazzling. The women seemed to be fashion models. The men seemed to be either millionaire lawyers or gorgeous young actors. And the bohemian element seemed to be German and French.

The food was delicious, the drinks never

ending, the hubbub a friendly drone punctuated by sudden laughter.

They found Krista's alley cat, Sweet William, stalking something among the bamboo stands.

They found her Chow bitch lying on her back on the third tier, being fed pâté and crackers by a ravishingly beautiful, anorectic, inebriated, six-foot-three-inch girl.

And then they found Gruesome. At first they both passed him by, thinking he was a piece of stone statuary. But then they noticed the leaf of lettuce hanging out of Gruesome's mouth.

"I have never seen a tortoise that big except in PBS specials on the Galapagos Islands," Didi noted.

"He doesn't seem to be eating that lettuce."

"He's thinking," Didi said. "Maybe they move so slow because they are thinking all the time. Maybe tortoises are not stupid. They're simply reflective. Or maybe they're like holy men along the river Ganges."

"I live in fear of Gruesome," Ilona admitted.

"Why?"

"Because one day Krista is going to ask me to sex Gruesome. I feel it in my bones. She's going to say, 'Ilona, is Gruesome a man or a woman?' Nightingale, tell me, do you know how to sex a tortoise?"

"I haven't the slightest idea."

"And we both graduated from the very best veterinary school in the world. How do you like them apples!"

Then Ilona wandered off to find some food. Didi headed toward the heart of the indoor forest. The bamboo trees, she realized, were set in tubs that were sunken beneath the floor and covered with some kind of moss. The flowering plants were arranged in riotous patterns on trellises, in hanging pots, and every which way.

It must take a small fortune to maintain such a garden, Didi thought. And it takes a whole lot of work. She wondered whether tortoises ate flowering plants.

She walked to the base of the greenhouse wall where the largest bamboo stands stood. The trees took one's breath away. Sinewy. Symmetrical. Ringed. Curving up and away from each other. A pale yellowish color that seemed to reflect moonlight.

Didi reached out and ran her hand slowly along one of the trees.

"Do not touch the merchandise!"

She pulled her hand back quickly and wheeled.

A man was standing off to her left. He was young, about thirty. He was lanky, dark complected, with a long face and black hair brushed straight back. He was wearing sandals, jeans, and an orange T-shirt that read in faded letters: I Don't Surf.

His right hand held a plate with an enormous pile of food. His left hand held two beer bottles. He seemed totally out of place, sartorially. But maybe not. He was quite relaxed.

"Who are you?" she asked.

"I've been hired as the game warden around here. In return for all these goodies."

He thrust the plate toward her, offering to share the food. She declined.

"Actually my name is Tor, and I'm not a game warden. I'm one of the new breed—a starving Soho sculptor. Who are you?"

"My name is Didi Nightingale. I'm a vet."

"Persian Gulf?"

"What?"

"Well, obviously you're too young for the Vietnam War."

"What are you talking about?"

"You said you're a vet. A veteran of what war?"

"No. I'm a veterinarian."

"Ah. A horse doctor."

"You can call me that."

"I once had a gecko. Boris. His name was Boris. He cleaned the roaches out from my loft. But then tragedy struck."

"What happened?"

"He just vanished. Poof! I believe he was kidnapped by a neighbor, on the floor below me. But a ransom note was never received."

He started in on his plate, balancing it precariously on one of the floral tubs.

Didi watched him. There was something about him that was starting to unnerve her. She wanted to leave, but she couldn't. It was that old fantasy coming back to haunt her. Didi had had only two affairs in her life. The first, in Philadelphia, with a professor. That had ended disastrously. The second, Allie Voegler. The man she was with now. But when she was alone and lonely, she would construct the man she wanted to meet . . . a lover . . . a fantasy . . . a theoretical construct. The fantasy changed from time to time—the man's looks and manner and biography—but always, yes always, for some reason he was always an artist, a sculptor, and he always lived in New York, in Soho. It was a harmless childish fantasy, but she could not shake it.

This is absurd, she thought.

She turned and started to walk away.

"Hey, where are you going?" he called out. "If you want to stroke some bamboo, go right ahead. I don't consider it much of a perversion."

Rose parked her car in front of the roadside office of Harold Brautigan, realtor. She had driven a few miles west out of Hillsbrook into Pleasant Valley on the hunch that local realtors were blasé.

Brautigan was at his desk and on the phone when she entered. He nodded hello. Rose Vigdor liked what she saw. He seemed substantial. He was well-dressed. He was clear-eyed. He sat erect behind his desk. And he wasn't that old.

He hung the phone up, leaned forward, folded his hands on the desk, and asked "What can I do for you?"

"My name is Rose Vigdor. I live in Hillsbrook and—"

He interrupted, stood up, proffered his hand, and said, "Call me Harry."

She shook his hand. He sat back down.

Rose thought, I must act very professionally. I must act like I was back in Manhattan . . . a full-blooded career woman.

"I have some property to sell," she said. "About three acres."

"Any road frontage?"

"About a hundred yards. Onto a county road. Then a field and a small stand of trees."

"And buildings on the property?"

"Not on those acres."

"Any water?"

"One pond. One well."

"Do you have a picture?"

"No."

He nodded, stared at her intently, leaned back, and clasped his hands behind his head. A sound outside caught his attention for a moment. But just for a moment. Then he looked back at her.

"Well now, Miss Vigdor, let me be honest. I'll list it. But between you and me, no one is buying land in Dutchess County anymore."

Rose was astonished at his pronouncement. When she recovered, she blurted out, "I'm talking about Hillsbrook acreage—prime, beautiful land."

"Please don't get upset, Miss Vigdor. I'm sure your parcel is beautiful. And Hillsbrook was always the place to buy if you could afford it. But right now—forget it! There's no market. First of all, taxes are too high. And then IBM moved out, so there's no more middle managers wandering about with $100,000 yearly salaries, ready to buy. To make matters worse—the downstate people aren't buying upstate acreage anymore since the IRS ended deductions for gentlemen farming operations."

Rose could not believe what she was hearing.

"It'll all turn around one day. But right now, believe me, no one is selling acreage. Because there are no buyers—at any price."

He paused. "You don't believe me, do you?"

Rose just held up her hands in confusion.

"Listen, let me give you a real-life example. A few months ago I get a call from a man who owns a small place on the Hudson . . . with a boating slip. Now the house on the property was kind of small and ramshackle . . . but so what? I mean, we're talking about Hudson River frontage. A beautiful spot. The man . . . I think his name was Farrah . . . no . . . wait . . . it was Schirra. That's right—Carl Schirra. He wanted to sell quick. I said sure. There will be no problem. Miss Vigdor, I didn't get a nibble. Not one. Then he takes the listing away from me."

Rose was silent.

"Do you see what I'm saying? Five years ago I would have had to beat off the potential buyers."

Rose walked out of the office in a daze and climbed into her car. She started to talk to her dogs, then realized she had left them back at the barn.

The realization that the real estate market had collapsed was bad enough. What disturbed her even more was that name . . . Carl Schirra. According to Mrs. Tunney, that was the name of the man who was shot to death in the nightclub.

The call came in for Didi as she was helping Ilona Baer drain an ear abscess on a fractious Manx cat named Pepper.

Didi took the call in the office. She was very happy to hear from her friend. Rose, as usual, talked over the phone in bursts—it was always a bit difficult to follow the gist of her conversation.

"Hello, girlfriend."

"Rose, I'm sorry I didn't contact you. Things just—"

"Forget it. Mrs. Tunney told me what happened. You always get into trouble, Doctor Nightgown. I think you need a full-time bodyguard. But, wait! You have one! I saw him parked by your house. The poor man is pining away for you. Wasting away, girlfriend. A hunk on a downward spiral."

Didi laughed. But she felt a twinge of bad faith. She should have called Allie. No doubt one of her elves told him what had happened. But she still should have called.

"Do I have news for you!"

And then Rose Vigdor told Didi about her visit to the Pleasant Valley real estate broker— the reason she made that visit—and the fortuitous unearthing of information on the man Didi had watched get shot to death.

Didi didn't know what to say. A lot of people owned cottages upstate. But it might mean something. One of the detectives, Phil Slater, had given all the eyewitnesses his card. She would call him.

Rose began to talk about how she was going to winterize her barn; about how she was relinquishing her Thoreau fantasy. As soon as she gets some money.

"How much do you need?"

"$5,000."

"Why didn't you ask me? I can scrape up the cash," Didi said, a bit hurt.

"I was about to . . . and I might do it anyway."

"We'll talk when I get back."

And Rose hung up. Didi rummaged in her wallet, found Slater's card, and made the call. A machine answered. She left a message detailing what Rose had told her, including the last name of the real estate agent.

Didi started back to the examining room. She saw the receptionist at the door of the office.

"You have another call," she said.

Didi turned back, saw the blinking light on another extension, and picked up.

"Hello!"

"Hello." It was an unfamiliar male voice.

"Is this the horse doctor?"

"What?"

"I'm the game warden."

"Wait a minute."

"Don't you remember my mellifluous voice? I'm the Triple S man from the party. Starving, Soho, Sculptor. But handsome. And talented. And oh so hip."

Didi remembered.

"I got your friend's number from Krista Michaels. What do two horse doctors talk about?"

"Geckoes," Didi quipped.

Tor found that hugely funny.

"The reason I'm calling, Doctor Nightingale, is that I demand you have a drink with me tomorrow night."

"Demand?"

"Yes. Otherwise, I will let it be known that I caught you in that most heinous of perverse acts—stroking bamboo. Your career will be ruined."

"We wouldn't want that to happen, would we?" Didi replied.

"The place is the Rawhide Bar. The time is 8:30. The dress is optional. The location is 9th Street and Avenue A."

"Is that in Soho?"

The caller laughed again. "So you really are a country bumpkin," he said. "No. It's in the

East Village. But that's the way it is. I live and work in Soho, but I party in the East Village."

"Is that what we're going to do—party?" Didi asked mischievously.

"We'll do anything you want."

He hung up. Didi felt absolutely stupid. Why had she said yes? And why the hell had she flirted like that? She headed back to the examining room. She remembered Rose's comments, about how she was going to bury her Thoreau fantasy and stay warm this coming winter.

Didi wondered why—if Rose could bury her fantasy—why couldn't she bury hers?

Chapter 4

It had been a very leisurely day so far for Charlie Gravis. All morning he had been snoozing in the small clinic attached to the big house. When a call came in, he would take down the information, then call the back-up vets.

But there had been only four calls.

A cow had run into some barbed wire.

Two goats were off their feed.

A riding horse might or might not have a touch of colic.

And two baby bats had been found in an apple orchard. What should be done with them?

At about noon Charlie went into the kitchen to get some lunch. Mrs. Tunney was gone. She had left a tuna sandwich and two Fig Newtons for him, along with a note saying that Trent Tucker had driven her into town to shop.

In the face of the tuna fish he lost his appetite. He did nibble one of the Fig Newtons.

Then he just sat on the kitchen chair and stared morosely out the screen door into the yard. The sky was darkening. And he could hear the rumble of thunder. One of those sudden midday midsummer storms was imminent, he realized.

But it came much faster than he imagined—and with a greater intensity. Suddenly, the sky became pitch black and the air became absolutely still. Then a rolling clap of thunder. Next, the lightning. And finally the rain. Slow at first, but as the thunder and lightning diminished, the rain intensified.

Charlie walked to the screen door and looked hard. It was a strange kind of rain. Light, dense sheets that whipped over the fields.

What did his father use to say about these rains? That it was Zeus pissing through a sieve.

Charlie smiled sadly. When his father would say that, Charlie was too embarrassed to admit that he didn't know what a sieve was.

Then he heard a strange sound cutting through the rain . . . like a buzz saw. Damn! It was the Doc's horse, Promise Me. He was whinnying crazily in the barn. That fool horse never liked storms.

Then came a more frightening sound. Promise Me was trying to kick down his stall.

Charlie grabbed one of the hats hanging on a wall hook and headed out the door into the rain. All he needed was for something to happen to the boss's darling while she was away.

He had gone about twenty feet when he saw Abigail coming from the other side of the house and heading toward the barn. Charlie cursed under his breath. What did Abigail know about crazed horses? She was going to get herself hurt. He noticed that she was wearing no rain gear whatsoever, and she was already drenched to the bone.

She vanished into the barn. The horse now seemed to be going absolutely bananas.

Charlie broke into a geriatric trot and finally reached the barn. He swung the doors wide open.

An astonishing sight greeted him. The big thoroughbred was rearing and whinnying in his stall, eyes wild, ears laid back.

Right in front of the stall was Abigail. Her eyes were closed, and her hands were behind her head, holding her long, wet golden hair.

Then she started to sing. It was, Charlie realized to his amazement, the old Negro spiritual "Go Down, Moses." This was not a hymn that was sung in their church. He had never heard Abigail sing it anywhere.

And she was singing it strangely . . . real light.

And when she reached the lines—let my people go—she sort of scatted it, like Ella Fitzgerald.

The horse stopped rearing. His ears and eyes relaxed. He gave a little snort.

Abigail kept singing.

There was another huge clap of thunder and the explosion of lightning close by. But Promise Me now looked bored. He went to his feed pail and began to munch.

Charlie slipped out of the barn and leaned against the door.

The rain was diminishing, and the sun was starting to peek through. Charlie took his rain hat off. Is it possible that strange, lovely Abigail is really some kind of witch? That's what he thought. Then he realized that was totally implausible. He started back to the house. Not plausible . . . but possible, he concluded.

Detectives Slater and Follette followed a few steps behind Arden Sellers as they walked out on the narrow concrete pier of the 79th Street Boat Basin fronting Riverside Park.

"There it is," Arden said, pointing to a squat, ugly houseboat moored at the end of the pier.

"How come you have a key?" Slater asked. The sun was hot, but unlike Follette, Phil Slater had not removed his jacket. He was thick across the stomach and self-conscious about it. He ran his hand through his thinning gray-black hair, now damp with sweat.

"Why shouldn't I have a key?" the young woman answered aggressively. "I was his number one bartender. I ran the damn place. He trusted me."

"With what?" Follette replied, a bit lewdly.

"And I don't understand why you're searching his place. Since when does the victim come under suspicion? You people seem to have everything backwards."

Both detectives ignored her comment. Follette stared out at the river. "I understand the fish are coming back here," he said. "I hear they are catching shad again only a few miles upriver."

Phil Slater made a face. He had always been less than happy with his partner. Follette lacked focus. He was lackadaisical. If he cleared a case, fine. If he didn't, fine also. His mind wandered. He didn't know which side his bread was buttered on.

"Do you also have a key to his upstate place?" Slater asked.

"What upstate place?"

"You didn't know he had a place just south of Kingston, on the river? Near the Kingston Bridge?"

"I wasn't aware of it," she replied.

Slater gave the young woman a cold look. She was difficult to read, he thought. Had they been lovers? Probably. Why the secrecy? Schirra wasn't married. He had already asked her that question: Had they slept together? He had asked it eight different ways, and he had gotten eight different evasive denials.

The simple fact was, Slater didn't believe Arden Sellers. Everything about her made him uneasy. He had the feeling she knew the killer. And he had the feeling that the blond shooter had also shared Schirra's bed.

The lock gave, the door swung open, and they walked into the dusty houseboat.

"Well, it sure isn't a yacht," Follette noted.

It was a depressing, one-room flat floating on water. That's all it was. The only bright thing was a gleaming new miniature wall kitchen in the rear.

"You take the closets," Slater said to his partner, then he walked to the dresser. It was one of those ancient green jobs that one used to run across in cheap downtown hotels, with two large knobs on either side of each drawer.

Slater went through the drawers. There was nothing but underwear and socks and a few rolled-up belts.

Then he walked to one of the two chests on either side of the bunk bed, opened it, rummaged through what could only be characterized as nautical junk—ropes, deflated life savers, lanterns, flares.

One item caught his attention, and he pulled it out. It was a rope ladder that had been coated with some kind of lubricating agent, now caked and dried. It intrigued him, but he didn't know why. He placed it on the bunk.

"Look!" Follette called out, holding a batch of weird hats. "The guy was a rain hat freak."

Slater moved to the next trunk. He glanced at the young woman. She had opened two of the windows and was now seated on the two-seat derelict sofa in front of the windows. She looked unhappy.

The second trunk was a festival of junk—tools, small cartons, large tattered envelopes with nothing in them, even ancient doilies.

He found a beautiful pair of English gardening shears.

He found a collection of old blues records.

And, in one of the envelopes, he found a few crude drawings that seemed to indicate Schirra had a passion for designing sandals.

He found several books on psychedelic drugs, old ones, including one Slater remembered from his youth, *Soma*, by Gordon Wasson.

He found two candlesticks with hunting motifs hammered into the brass.

And he found a whole lot more, none of it seemingly relevant.

He stepped away from the trunk and straightened up slowly. His back was beginning to hurt.

"Didn't he have a desk?"

Arden replied: "No desk. What you see is what you get."

"No photographs. No letters," Slater said. "That doesn't make sense. We went through his office in Boots. No letters or photographs there, either. It doesn't make sense."

"Maybe he was shy," Arden said.

"Hey look!" Follette was walking toward him, holding something. "I found this in a corduroy jacket." He laid the object on the bunk bed.

It was a thick stack of road maps fastened by several rubber bands.

Slater removed the rubber bands.

"New York State road maps," Follette noted.

"He didn't have a car," Slater replied.

"So he rented."

Slater opened all six of them. Each one was a county map. Orange, Ulster, and Greene counties on the west bank of the Hudson. And Putnam, Dutchess, and Columbia counties on the east bank.

"Not your usual maps," Slater said.

"What do you mean?"

"I mean they're very detailed. Salesmen use these. You get them in those travel bookstores like Hagstrom's and Rand-McNally."

He gestured for Arden Sellers to join them. She came over slowly.

"You ever see these before?" Slater asked her.

She picked up one and studied it. She looked at the others. "No."

"Sure?"

"I'm sure."

"Maybe he just liked to collect upstate maps," Follette suggested. "Like he did rain hats. Anyway, he did have a place up there. Who knows? A direction problem? Maybe he had a hard time identifying direction. There are people like that. Did you ever take a compass course in the Army, Phil?"

Slater didn't answer. He stacked the maps neatly and placed the rubber bands back on them.

This Schirra was a cipher, he thought. No letters. No photographs. And no bank books or bank statements of any kind. Everything simple. Everything bare. Except the trunks, which had inexplicable junk like fancy gardening shears. He heard Follette start to question the Sellers girl again. Follette was bearing down. He wanted an exact accounting of her visits to the houseboat—when, how often, and the circumstances of each visit. Slater didn't interrupt his partner, but he wasn't really listening.

Didi stood on the corner of St. Marks and Avenue A across from Tompkins Square Park. She was in a kind of shock. Yes, she had heard of the East Village, and she had read about it, but she had never expected such a density of people.

And what strange, wonderful people they were!

She had her eye on one particular table in one sidewalk cafe just west of Avenue A. Four young people were seated at the table, smoking. There was a tall, absolutely ravishing young woman with orange hair and unshod feet. Another girl with rings in her ears and nose. A bald man in an expensive suit with no shirt underneath. The fourth individual was or seemed to be a biker. He wore a leather vest that bared his midriff, was heavily muscled, had long scruffy hair, and his body was completely tattooed. On his right arm, running from elbow to wrist was a particularly horrendous conglomeration of entwined gargoyles.

The night was moonless, yet the streets seemed to create their own kind of light. Didi smiled. I am in the East Village to meet a man in a bar. What would Rose say? Oh, something like—turn a country vet loose in the big city and you know she'll turn into a wild thang.

It's strange, Didi thought, how comfortable I feel here in this crowd of young people who would probably rather die than live in Hillsbrook.

But when she turned up Avenue A to the corner of 9th Street and walked into the Rawhide Bar, her comfort level diminished rapidly. This is not a place to be, she immediately thought.

The people at the bar and the booths were much older and grimmer, and their clothes were funky but without panache. Who were they? Old poets? Old junkies? Were they lost? Were they damned?

She looked for the sculptor. He was nowhere to be seen.

Suddenly, Patsy Cline's "Crazy" came on the jukebox. Didi felt a little bit better. How bad can a place be if they're playing Patsy!

A hand reached out and touched her arm. She jumped.

"Relax, Doc." It was Tor. Didi laughed nervously.

"The bar, madame? Or a booth?" he asked with mocking politeness.

"Your choice," she said.

He led her to the far end of the bar. There was one stool open. Didi sat down. Tor stood beside her. She ordered a stein of ale. He ordered a rum and orange juice. The bar was thick with smoke. The juke box, now behind them, was into Willie Nelson. Why so much country music? Didi thought.

"I like calling you Doc . . . do you mind?"

"Not really. I hate the name Deirdre, anyway."

"Why?"

"Because Deirdre always gets contracted to Didi, and you end up sounding like the neighbor on a sitcom. Actually, people calling me Didi never bothered me. Although, to be quite honest, I always wanted to be named Adriana. Don't ask me why."

The ale was ice cold and delicious.

She looked straight at him. "What's your last name?"

"Torvald."

"Oh. Then what's your first name?"

"Torvald."

"You're putting me on."

"No. I am now legally named Torvald. One name. Just like Michelangelo. Everyone called him Mickey. Everyone calls me Tor."

She laughed and drank more of the ale. The foam speckled the side of the mug. Didi kept staring at the bartender—a woman with long hair wrapped in braids around her head. She kept snatching up money from the bar like a robin plucking up worms.

"What kind of stuff do you do?" Didi asked. His closeness was unnerving her. She felt the question to be foolish, almost aggressive, but it just popped out. She did want to talk to him. The whole situation felt illicit.

"Collages."

"Collages?"

"Things you know. Objects in space. I'm working with glass and wood now. I like them. Wood splinters and glass shatters. You know what I mean?"

"Vaguely," Didi said. She looked away from him. The moment he started talking about his work he looked different . . . a bit less humorous . . . a bit less wild. He was serious about his work if about nothing else. Didi shook her head. She could not believe she was really sitting in a raunchy bar in the East Village with a real live Soho sculptor.

"Why don't you buy some of my stuff?" Tor asked.

"I've never even seen it."

"But if you saw it and liked it . . . then would you buy it?"

"A few days ago, maybe. But now a friend of mine needs $5,000, and that's about all the cash I have on hand."

"I thought you vets make millions," he said.

"Now *that's* a sitcom."

He leaned over and whispered in her ear. "Damn! I thought you were rich. I thought you were going to take care of me."

She pushed him away gently. "That'll be the day."

The juke box started on Otis Redding. That was fine with Didi.

"Let's get out of here," he said.

"Where to?"

"I know a nicer bar, not too far from here."

They left and made their way to a teeming, lively bar on Ludlow Street. Then to a bar in Tribeca. Then to a coffee shop in Soho. They were getting along fine. They were laughing. They were loose. Didi forgot where the hell she came from and where the hell she was going. The city made her drunk.

As for Tor, he kept pumping her for funny or bizarre vet stories—and she remembered several and she recounted them. He laughed at anything concerning goats.

"What is this thing you have with goats?"

She stirred some Sweet 'n Low into her iced tea.

He shrugged at the question in a slightly inebriated fashion. Then he shook his hair like a wet dog. Then he leaned back in his chair and said, "I believe that a feverish goat is the closest one can come to wisdom."

"Amen," Didi replied.

"Amen," Tor mimicked, then he dropped his head down on the table and rested there.

Didi sipped the tea and smiled. She wasn't doing anything wrong in enjoying herself. She liked this offbeat young man. She still loved Allie Voegler. But she liked Tor. Big deal. And the places he had taken her . . . ah . . . she loved the bars. And she loved the strange people. Above all, she loved the way they dressed . . . with a passion. It was a whole different world. But oddly her own. Did she wish Allie were here now? She couldn't answer that question.

Tor was staring at her, his head still down on the table. "You're very beautiful, Nightingale. I have fallen in love with you."

"You'll get over it," Didi said. "I'm taken."

"Good. Now you can come up to my loft and objectively evaluate my stuff and admit after careful observation that I am truly the most innovative and important sculptor you have ever encountered in your world of goats."

"I can't. I have to get back."

"Back where? There's nowhere to go, Dr. Nightingale. You're a stranger in a strange land."

"So I am. But I don't feel that way at all."

"Look at me, Doc."

"I am looking."

"Do I appear drunk?"

"A bit."

"Do I appear dangerous?"

"Not at all."

"Good." He got to his feet and held out his hand. "I want your opinion. I want it very much."

So Didi went to his loft with him—a marvelous space on Greene Street just north of Canal, at the rear of the third floor.

He flipped the light switch on and Didi stared around in wonderment.

Yes . . . he worked in wood and glass . . . but she had never seen pieces like this. There were fifteen or twenty of his works along the spine of the loft. The base of each piece was a large wooden door—old, cracked, peeling—obviously obtained from a Dumpster where a house was being renovated and the old doors thrown away.

Attached to each door in a wide variety of patterns were old wineglasses and water glasses, probably obtained from thrift stores or garage sales. Many of the glasses seemed to be chipped or cut by the sculptor himself to establish some kind of . . . Didi didn't know what.

Most of the doors were on stands at 45 degree angles. But some of the doors were simply standing up or flat on the ground.

In three or four of the pieces he had painted the glasses eerie colors of red and gray and yellow.

It was like being in a different kind of bamboo forest. Didi walked slowly back and forth among the pieces.

Tor went to a small refrigerator, took out

some ice cubes, and rubbed them along his neck. "Well? What do you think?"

"I think they're amazing."

"I knew you would. So you do love me, Doc?"

"No. I love your work. I don't love you."

"Why persist in this charade?" he asked, laughing.

"What charade?"

He didn't answer. He walked over and offered Didi some ice cubes. She let him drop one in her palm.

Then he grabbed her and kissed her. She turned her face away from him.

"Let me go," she said hoarsely. His grip hurt.

He laughed and said in a low tone that matched hers, "I will never let you go." He laughed again, crazily. "I am your feverish goat."

"Let me go, you drunken idiot!"

"But I'm not drunk, Doc. I'm—"

She lifted her foot and drove it savagely down to the top of his arch. He cried out and released his grip, staggering backwards.

Didi turned and strode to the door. She was enraged . . . at everything . . . at him . . . at herself for being so stupid as to go to his loft . . . at her pathetic inability to shake her fantasy . . . at her relationship with Allie . . . at the world.

She lashed out with her hands as she walked.

Two of the pieces came off their stands. The glasses shattered. She slammed the door behind her.

They were driving up the Taconic Parkway with Detective Follette at the wheel. Slater was trying to nap.

"I don't see the point of this," Follette said, "though it is a damn nice road."

"There is no point," Slater said wearily. Then he laughed. "But this Schirra character didn't have any point either. He's just dead. And this is one of the places he lived in. So we take a look. Looking is the point; if there is one."

"Those maps we found in the closet still bug me," Follette said, "but I can't figure out what they're about."

"They are weird," Slater agreed. "But everything about Schirra is kind of weird . . . by omission, if you know what I mean. For example, I've been in this business a long time, and I used to work in vice. Believe me, I met a lot of nightclub owners, cabaret owners, bar and grill owners. You name it. And I never met one that wasn't in some kind of trouble."

"You mean money trouble?" Follette asked, not taking his eyes off the road.

"Right. Loan-shark trouble. Bank trouble. Tax trouble. Licensing trouble. But not this Schirra. I asked around. No one knows anything about him, or his place, Boots."

"It looked like a nice joint to me," Follette said.

"They had some good acts over the years. At least so I've been told. And the place was clean."

Then Slater said, "Do me a favor and turn that stupid air conditioner off."

His partner flipped the switch. Slater opened his window all the way. It was hot out. Follette lowered the driver's side window.

"Schirra is like quicksilver," Slater complained. "And that blond shooter is no better. She arrives in a bike messenger outfit. But she has no bike and no messenger company in the city can ID her. She arrives with a bouquet of roses. But no florist in the city sold them to her. You figure it out."

They drove the next ten miles in silence.

"The turnoff is soon," Slater said.

"How did we learn about his upstate place?"

"That lady vet heard it from a friend. She called me. I called an agent whose name she also gave me—a real estate agent named Brautigan. Schirra listed the place with him once. Brautigan gave me the location. It's next to a Catholic nursing home for old priests. Schirra, it seems, threw the handyman there—name of Hardaway—a few bucks each month to watch his place."

"I like that lady vet," Follette said. Slater didn't comment.

"We had a conversation," Follette replied. "At the bar. The day of the shooting. I think she liked me."

"How do you know that?"

"You know. Just a feeling."

"She's out of your league," Slater said.

"You think what you want to think," Follette replied testily.

They turned off the highway and five minutes later pulled up in front of the nursing home. It had obviously once been a mansion. The lawns were still monumental and well kept, sweeping down toward the cliffs and the river below. The patients were visible, scattered throughout the grounds in wheelchairs, on crutches, or using their own feeble legs. There was, oddly, an air of efficiency about the place.

Peter Hardaway, the caretaker, was unimpressed by the NYPD credentials the two detectives flashed at him. He treated them with suspicion, like tradesmen, but he led them to Schirra's place.

It abutted the nursing home property, but it was only a sliver of land—a kind of grassy sliver that sloped down to the river between two cliffs.

"A quarry started up here," Peter explained. "They destroyed a chunk of cliffs, then packed the whole operation in. I'm talking about the 1890s."

It was an ugly little clapboard cottage. Peter opened the door for them, said "God rest his soul," and started to leave.

Slater stopped him with the artist's sketch of the shooter. "Do you know her?" he asked.

"No!" said Hardaway.

"You never saw anyone like her up here?"

"No. I never saw anyone up here. Not even

Mr. Schirra, except once in a long while. But I don't look in often."

Hardaway walked away. He called back once. "Make sure the door is closed when you leave." Slater noticed that he limped badly going uphill.

The two detectives stared morosely around. The houseboat had been minimally furnished. But this cottage was absolutely bare. No furniture except one chair, one sleeping mat, one portable clothing rack, and a great variety of brooms and mops and snow shovels. The closet was empty except for old shoes. The kitchen cabinet was empty, and the water turned off.

"No mercy," Slater said. He took a small penknife from his pocket, opened it, and slit the little mat open. "You have to be thorough in these matters," he said sardonically. Then he ripped open the linings of the three items on the portable clothing rack.

There was nothing but wisps of fabric floating through the air.

The thorough search was over.

They stood silently in the center of the cottage, the heat closing in on them.

Finally, Follette picked up one of the brooms and began to bang it against a wall.

"What the hell are you doing?" Slater demanded.

"Looking for hidden storage areas."

"Not too funny."

Follette flung the broom across the room. They walked out, down the slope, and right up to the river bank. On either side of them were cliffs. The boating slip had decayed to such a degree that only its outline appeared above water, like a sunken hulk.

Slater sat down on the ground and lit a cigarette. The condition of the slip matched the condition of this investigation. Well, he thought, at least it proved that Follette could be right at least once in a while. The trip had been idiotic.

"Now what?" Follette inquired.

"We go back up the slope. We go into the nursing home and show the sketch to everyone with functioning eyes. Then we go back to the cottage, pick up broom handles, and search for hidden storage areas."

Follette did not know how to take that. So he said nothing.

A noise woke Didi. She sat straight up. It

had been Ilona closing the door behind her, leaving the apartment for the clinic.

Didi walked into the living room. The sun through the windows stunned her.

Ilona's customary note was there—about coffee and muffins in the kitchen, about coming down to the clinic when she got up.

But there were another few lines on the note this morning:

> You used to be such a good little girl in vet school, Nightingale. You never came home at 2 in the morning.

Didi didn't think it was funny. She went into the kitchen, poured half a cup of still warm coffee into a mug, and sat down at the kitchen table. She didn't want to think about last night. It was too ugly, too pathetic.

She put some sugar in the mug. The coffee was horrible. She walked to the sink and poured it out. A headache was forming . . . and Didi could tell it was going to be a whopper.

She turned on the flame under the coffee, waited a few minutes impatiently, then poured herself another cup.

She sat back down at the table. She took one

sip of the hot coffee, grimaced, pushed the cup away, and lay her head down on the table.

It is time to go home, she realized. *Not* this afternoon . . . *not* tonight. *Now!*

She looked at the clock on the kitchen wall—a big clock with iridescent hands. It was too late to make the morning train, but there was an Amtrak special around noon. She could call either Trent Tucker or Allie from Grand Central, just before the train left, and one of them could pick her up.

She rushed into the guest room to pack, and she packed with a fury. Then she went into the living room, found several envelopes and wrote a note to Ilona.

Something came up in my practice. Not serious but I have to get back. Thanks for everything. Will call you soon. Love, Nightingale.

Then, suitcase in hand, she walked toward Grand Central. The closer she got to the terminal, the slower her stride became. And her passion to get out of Manhattan diminished. She began to think clearly about what had transpired, at least trying to deal rationally with what happened.

There was no doubt the sculptor had made a pass at her and reinforced it with a physical presence. He had tried to intimidate her physically.

But the pass itself—wasn't that to be expected? Why had she been stupid enough to go up to the loft with him when he was clearly inebriated?

As she walked and thought, the incident seemed to lose a great deal of the horror it had elicited from her in the morning.

As she approached the terminal, in fact, it was her behavior rather than that fool's behavior that was beginning to horrify her. Because, like it or not, she had destroyed some of his work. She had deliberately, in her fury at being grabbed, knocked over and shattered several pieces of Tor's art work.

That was, she realized, stopping dead in her tracks only a block from the terminal, a terrible thing to do. She had never done anything remotely like that before in her life. It was something she never believed herself capable of . . . no matter the provocation.

She reached the terminal. I have to call him,

she thought. I have to apologize for what I did. There was no excuse.

No, she decided, it would be better simply to go down there now, talk to him, confront him with what had happened, apologize, get his apology, and part like two adults in good faith. There was a later train. She walked into Grand Central, checked her bag in one of the lockers, and took a cab down to Canal and Greene.

The cab driver let her out at the corner of Grand and Greene. Didi started to protest. But then she saw that she was only half a block from Tor's place, so she climbed out of the cab and started to fumble for payment.

As the cab driver was handing her her change, Didi saw Tor emerging from his building. It was an astonishing bit of luck. The cab drove off. Didi raised her hand and was just about to call out when she saw that Tor was not alone. Another man had come out of the building with him. They had crossed the street and would now pass her on the other side of the street heading toward Grand.

Didi watched them. She didn't call out. She didn't wave. She stared at the man with Tor.

He was so familiar . . . so shatteringly familiar. But she couldn't put a name to the face.

They turned the corner. Didi started after them. Then she stopped suddenly. She knew who that young man was. His name was Darryl Yates, and he had been in the audience at Boots on the night of the murder. He had been doing a crossword puzzle.

She looked around for a bar or restaurant. Suddenly, she had to sit down.

Chapter 5

"What's the matter with you?" Mrs. Tunney asked Charlie Gravis, who was standing in the hallway that led from the clinic office to the kitchen.

"Nothing's the matter," he replied.

"You look like a little boy who lost his pet toad."

Charlie seemed to mull over the comparison in silence for a long while. Finally, he said, "Seeing how I've spent all morning answering stupid telephone calls and that I have about eleven dollars in cash to my name, I think I'm looking pretty good."

"Stop feeling sorry for yourself, Charlie. You have your health. You want some iced tea?"

"No. I'm going for a walk."

Mrs. Tunney let out a whoop of sarcastic

laughter. "Charlie Gravis going for a walk? You haven't done that in twenty years."

Charlie walked right past her without another word, went out the screen door, headed around the north side of the house, cursing the yard dogs who mobbed him, and then turned up the road, walking slowly on the already hot tar.

He turned in on Job's Lane and stopped when he came abreast of the ramshackle general store called Mother's. It used to be called Hillsbrook Service, and before that it was called Harold's, and before that . . . Charlie couldn't remember.

He stared at the store. He grinned. The fact was, he knew, that this had been his destination in the first place, but he sure as hell couldn't admit it to Tunney. After all, he was a recovering alcoholic, or so they said . . . yes . . . they all said that Charlie hadn't had a drink in thirty years. But it was nonsense. He still drank beer whenever he could . . . not the hard stuff . . . but beer certainly. And that was what he wanted now—a long ice-cold bottle of German beer.

Charlie walked inside, greeted the girl behind the counter, went to the fridge, took out the first bottle he saw with a German name, paid for it, used the opener that hung from the counter, and then walked out back to the porch. This was where it was traditional to drink the beer. This was where the dairy farmers used to congregate.

There were three men already on the porch, taking up all the existing chairs. But none of them were dairy people. They greeted Charlie warmly but not by name. Charlie knew them all . . . but not by name. One was a milk buyer from the yogurt plant about twenty miles north. And the other two were feed salesmen.

Charlie leaned against the railing, took a long swallow, and concentrated on the yellow-jackets buzzing along the wood.

One of the feed salesmen, a youngish man wearing a white sport shirt and a loosened tie, was talking about his visit to a dairy farmer named Badian. Charlie's ears pricked up. This had to be his old friend Ike Badian, the only one Charlie knew his age who still ran a working dairy operation.

". . . Anyway, so I walk over to him and start talking. He's leaning against a fence, chewing an unlit cigar."

Charlie smiled to himself. Yes, that was Ike all right.

"I do a very simple, but if I must say so myself, a very thorough presentation about our new supplements . . . about their nutritional value . . . about how they are safely integrating hormones . . . you know . . . the whole story. He listens and keeps nodding. From time to time he spits out pieces of the cigar. The man never lights it. Just chews it.

"When I'm finished, I pause, like they taught me in sales class, for dramatic effect, and I give him the punch line. I say that these new supplements are guaranteed to increase milk yield in each and every cow in the herd."

The feed man took a long drink from his Miller can. He wiped his mouth with a handkerchief.

"So," he continued, "this Badian waits a long time before answering, and then he says, 'The way I see it is this: When they want to let their milk down, they do. They let down what they want, when they want. But thanks for stopping by.' "

The other salesman found this hilarious. The milk buyer didn't. "A lot of the old characters think it's smart to act like a primitive. But don't underestimate them. I know they all use that saying—it's been around for a hundred years—letting the milk down. But listen, they know damn well each individual cow has absolutely no control over her yield. It's all physiological and hormonal and they know it."

The feed salesman who thought the story hilarious broke out into a kind of lewd variation on "letting the milk down."

It reminded Charlie of that line Abigail had sung in the barn during the storm . . . the line she had scatted from the old Negro spiritual "Go Down, Moses."

Charlie finished his beer, nodded good-bye, and walked back down the road. He walked very slowly, ruminating over the conversation he had just heard. He dimly remembered something from thirty years back, during his last years as a dairy farmer, when he had become interested in increasing milk yield in order to survive falling milk prices and skyrocketing feed costs. But the specifics eluded him.

Didi looked at the clock. It was almost one. She had been sitting in a dingy pizza parlor on the corner of Grand Street and Broadway for more than an hour. The two men behind the counter had started to stare at her suspiciously. She went up to the counter and finally ordered a slice and a Coke. She brought the items back to the table, but just stared at them.

What was Tor doing with Darryl Yates? How did they know each other? What did it mean? Of course, she realized, it could be total coincidence. Or could it have something to do with Krista Michaels? Tor obviously knew her; he had been a guest at her party. And Krista had once gone with Carl Schirra. But Yates had just wandered into Boots to see a show. He probably didn't know Krista at all. The whole thing was confusing. More than confusing, Didi thought. It was a bit frightening. But she could not say exactly why.

At the back of the pizza parlor were two gleaming pay phones. Why didn't she call Torvald? Why didn't she just ask him for an explanation? It could be quite a simple one. And then she could apologize for what she had done. And he could apologize. And she could go back to Hillsbrook, and all's well that ends well.

She stared at the phone. She realized that she also just simply wanted to talk to him again. Oh my, she thought, chagrined, how these childhood fantasies of love and adventure persist. They die hard.

She set out three quarters from her coin purse on the table. She closed her eyes for a moment and calmed herself. A memory surfaced—of a man standing on a small stage, arguing with the young woman who had brought new flowers. And then the sound of the gun shot. And then the man falling and the chaos and the microphone hitting the floor.

And herself, like a frightened child, falling to the floor in fear and bruising her palms. Why hadn't she gone after the murderer?

Didi gathered the quarters and walked to the phone. She had two options. Call information and get Krista Michaels's number. Or see if Tor had a listing. She opted for Krista. Information gave her the number of a K. Michaels on West End Avenue. She called, and a machine answered. Didi hung up without leaving a message. Then she tried Information on the sculptor. Good luck. Yes, there was a listing for a T. Torvald on Greene Street.

She called the number. A machine picked up there, too. She left her name and said she would call back in twenty minutes. She returned to the table and took a bite of the pizza slice. It was different from the Hillsbrook pizza Trent Tucker was always bringing into the house up there. It had much less cheese and a much thinner crust. It wasn't bad.

She called back in fifteen minutes. Tor answered on the first ring with an aggressive "Yes?"

For some reason Didi couldn't reply. A tremor started in her legs.

"Yes? Yes?" Tor was practically shouting into the phone.

"It's me," she finally replied.

"Who's me?"

"Didi . . . Dr. Nightingale."

He was silent. They were both silent.

She said, "I'm going back to Hillsbrook. I just wanted to say how sorry I was for the pieces I wrecked. You deserved some kind of punishment, but not that."

"Just some glass and some wood," he said in a surly voice. Then he asked, "Did I hurt you when I grabbed you?"

"No."

"Things just got out of control. You were standing there. And I just wanted to hold you."

"You were drunk, Tor."

"I imagine I was."

She knew what she had to do next—set the hook. But she hesitated. Why was she still fascinated with this fool who had physically abused her? Then Didi did what she had to do.

"Actually, Tor, I didn't want to phone. I wanted to talk to you face-to-face. I took a cab down to Greene Street. I saw you coming out of the building. I started over, but then I saw you were with someone and I didn't want to embarrass you."

"Are you talking about just before . . . about an hour or so ago?"

"Yes."

"That was just an old friend visiting. We used to work together as preparators."

"As what?"

"Preparators. We set up exhibits in galleries. He still does that. His name is Johnny Baum."

Didi didn't reply. Tor said, "Look, Doc, do me a favor. The next time you come to the big city, call me. I want another chance."

"That's fine with me," Didi said. She hung up the phone. She stood there, a very bad taste in her mouth. Tor had lied flat out. She knew who that young man was . . . Darryl Yates . . .

and she had heard he owned a trucking company.

Didi walked out of the pizza parlor and took a cab to Grand Central. She collected her valise and took another cab to Ilona's apartment. She was running out of cash.

Ilona was reading her note when she walked in.

"What's going on, Nightingale? You don't show up at the clinic, so finally I come up. I find this note that you left. I look up and here you are again. Are you going around the bend, Nightingale?"

Didi laughed and sat down. "The problem at home turned out to be not such a big problem. So I didn't take the train."

"Good! It was too soon for you to leave."

Ilona came over and kissed her on the head. "Besides, an old friend is waiting for you downstairs."

"Who?"

"A surprise. Unpack and come on down." Then Ilona ran out, tearing up Didi's note flamboyantly as she exited.

Didi leaned back and rested. She didn't unpack yet. She went into the opulent bathroom, showered, and changed into fresh jeans.

Then she called Detective Phil Slater. Again the machine. She left a message that she had to see him immediately and he should come to Ilona's apartment about four if possible. She had information pertaining to the Schirra murder.

Then she went down to the clinic. The moment she entered the examining room, Ilona called out, "Didn't I tell you an old friend was here?"

All Didi could see was the assistant, Harky, and a cat on one of the examining tables.

"Don't you recognize him?" said Ilona. "It's Sweet William."

Yes. Now she remembered; Krista Michaels's thuggish alley cat, who was hunting something in that indoor garden grove.

"Krista dropped him off. He's suddenly feeling very poorly. It may be FIA."

Didi walked close to the table. Sweet William looked very weary. He snarled at her, but just a bit. He was obviously out of sorts.

Didi treated few cats in her upstate practice. But she was fascinated by them and wanted to know more—one of the reasons she wanted to work with Ilona. She scratched Sweet William on the back of his neck. Her book learning about FIA flooded back into memory. Feline Infectious Anemia—a major disorder caused by the parasite haemobartonella felis. The clinical signs can include fever, jaundice, anorexia, depression, weakness, emaciation, enlarged spleen and lymph nodes. Diagnosis requires lab confirmation of presence of parasite in peripheral blood or bone marrow. Treatment includes transfusion and/or administration of tetracycline hydrochloride. Yes, she remembered at least part of what she had learned in vet school.

"The lab work is being done now," Ilona announced.

Didi stayed in the examining room until 3:45, then returned to the apartment.

Detective Slater arrived at two minutes past four, alone.

The moment he sat down on the sofa, he said, "This air-conditioning is brutal. Why do you keep it so cold?"

Didi laughed apologetically. "I'm just a visitor here. Besides, I haven't the foggiest notion how to adjust it."

She liked this detective. He seemed honest, blunt, grizzled. He reminded her of an FDA inspector checking out sanitary milking processes.

"What do you have for me?" he asked. Before Didi could say a word, he added, "Let me thank you for that call about Schirra's place upstate. My partner and I checked it out."

Didi nodded. She asked, "Does the name Krista Michaels ring a bell?"

"Sure. We interviewed her. She used to go with Schirra. She wasn't much help."

"I went to a party there, a few nights ago. I met a sculptor, a man who calls himself Tor. He claimed to use only that one name, Torvald."

Slater held up one hand, signaling that she should hold up. He pulled out a small notebook and a mechanical pencil. He wrote the name Torvald down. He nodded for her to continue.

"He called me. I went out with him on a date. It got ugly at the end. He mauled me. I smashed some of his art, then I left. This morning I decided to go home. On the way to the train station, I stopped off to apologize for the damage I did. I saw him walking with Darryl Yates."

"Really? The same Yates who—"

"Yes. So I called him."

"You mean this Torvald?"

"Yes. I told him I'd seen him on the street with someone and asked him who his friend was. He gave me a phoney name and said Yates had some kind of job in the art gallery world."

Slater was silent. He seemed to be doodling in his notebook.

Didi pressed. "Has the name Torvald come up at all in your investigation?"

"No."

"Could you put surveillance on him?"

Slater suppressed a smile. "This thing you call surveillance, Dr. Nightingale, is a very expensive proposition. The department doesn't go into it lightly. You know . . . how can I put it? There are eight million coincidences in the naked city; this just may be one of them."

Didi gave him a strange look.

"*Naked City,*" he said.

"What?"

"Didn't you ever see that television cop show, *Naked City*? Or maybe you saw it in reruns."

"No. I never heard of it."

"How old are you?"

"Twenty-nine."

"I guess it was way before your time. Anyway, I stole that line from the show. Each episode would end with a voice-over, 'There are eight million stories in the naked city. This has been one of them.' "

"Oh. Well, Detective Slater, I don't think it is a coincidence. I think I stumbled onto something."

"Maybe," he allowed.

He stood and thanked her. He made another nasty comment about the air-conditioning, then he left. Didi fell fast asleep on the sofa.

"We close in forty-five minutes," the librarian in the Hillsbrook Public Library said in response to Charlie Gravis's question. Then she added, "The hours, by the way, are posted clearly on the door."

"At my age, nothing is clear," Charlie replied, trying a little humor.

"What can I do for you?" the woman asked. She was quite attractive. Charlie wondered whether she lived in Hillsbrook; she didn't seem familiar at all. Of course, he hadn't been in this library in twenty years. Why? He didn't read, except for newspapers.

"I'm looking for back issues of a magazine."

"Well, right down the hall there is the periodicals room. On the left. Across from the water fountain. We don't really collect periodicals anymore. And we discontinued all the popular magazines."

"Why's that?" Charlie asked, curious.

"It's called cost reduction in the budget."

"I heard of him," Charlie said, his second attempt at humor, also unsuccessful.

"The fiche readers are in there, but the fiche rolls are stored on the second floor. So you just jot down what you want and bring the slip to me."

Charlie looked at her blankly. He hadn't the faintest idea what she was talking about. Something about fish . . . or fiche. What was fiche? Ah well. He thanked her and walked down the hall into the periodicals room. He saw strange-looking machines there. He saw computers. He saw catalogues with products he didn't recognize. He saw five immense reading tables.

Other than himself, only one other human was in the room—a Hillsbrook barber named Larry. He waved at Charlie, who waved back. Larry was reading an old magazine in a binder.

Yes! Charlie thought. That is what I am looking for, binders. If they had the *New York Dairy-man*, it would now be in a binder on a shelf under either "New York" or "Dairyman." The journal hadn't lasted more than five or six years, if he remembered correctly.

Charlie entered the shelves area. High and forbidding, they were. The floor was covered with a raspy carpet that seemed to suck his feet down.

But he found them. Oh yes. They lay undisturbed on a shelf, filed under "New York." A binder for each of the five years the magazine was published—1964, 1965, 1966, 1967, 1968. And each binder held six semimonthly issues.

He lugged all five binders back to a table. Larry had vanished. The problem was time, Charlie realized. He couldn't go through all thirty issues in the forty or so minutes the library would remain open. Of course, he could come back the next day. Or the next. But it was always best to strike while the iron was hot.

He opted for the flip and peek method.

He stood the 1964 binder upright and began to flip the pages the way he used to flip cards as a kid. He gambled that even his old eyes would pick up a distinctive headline or illustration or photograph and transmit to memory.

The gamble paid off. Halfway through the 1967 volume, his eyes fell on something. But his flipping had carried him far past the eye contact. So he had to upend the binder and go back laboriously, page by page.

Then . . . victory! There it was. The headline read:

BEETHOVEN IN THE BARN?

The article related how scientists now believe that the best way to increase yield is to make the cows happier. And how several experiments at Midwest land-grant universities point to the effectiveness of music in the barn to increase the contentment and yield of the milk cows.

Charlie closed the binder. He was ecstatic. He felt like rolling on top of the table. It had been—this Beethoven in the barn—a fad in the dairy world. It had come and gone. To be replaced by nutritional fads and hormonal fads and God knows what else.

But now the past was going to rear up and bite. And bring the bacon home.

I could kiss her, Charlie thought as he waved good-bye to the librarian.

Chapter 6

Allie Voegler went to bed at four in the afternoon. He had an erotic dream about Miss Nightingale, and he woke at six. He had two swigs of cold orange juice and went back to bed at 6:20. He had a nightmare about Leavis, the Hillsbrook chief of police, Allie's boss. He woke again at eight. He went right back to sleep.

And he slept until 11:05, when the phone woke him.

This time he would not get back to sleep. It was Officer Chung calling. He wanted to come up. He said he had some news.

Chung was climbing the stairs to Allie's place twenty minutes later. Allie sat on the bed and listened to the uniformed officer's story.

Chung has a friend on the Kingston police

force, he said. He met him for a few drinks tonight. The friend had just come off duty. The Kingston cops found a body at the base of the cliffs just south of the bridge. A woman. Young. From downstate. Name of Arden Sellers. She had been rock climbing. Nothing suspicious. Kingston cops probably bag ten bodies a year—kids climbing who shouldn't.

Chung paused long enough in the telling of his disjointed story to get a beer from Allie's refrigerator without asking.

"What does all this have to do with me?" Allie asked when Chung was seated again.

"The body had a slip of paper—folded—in a pocket. There was a name and number on it: Trent Tucker was the name. The phone number was Nightingale's.

Allie cursed.

"That's all," Chung said. "I just thought you'd want to know."

"What was the girl's last name again?"

"Arden Sellers."

Chung finished the beer and left. Allie dressed. It was his responsibility to look after Didi's elves when she was gone, in spite of the fact that they didn't like him and the feeling was mutual. And this sounded like a problem. Trent Tucker was always a problem.

He drove to the Nightingale house. No lights were on. The moment he climbed out of the car, the yard dogs surrounded him, yapping, the hall light went on, and then Mrs. Tunney opened the door.

"Who is that?"

"Allie Voegler."

"Dr. Nightingale's away."

"I know that. I want to see Trent Tucker."

"Why don't you come back in the morning?"

"No, sorry. Now!" And he just walked in past her.

Trent was on his bed in his tiny room, listening to music on earphones. The kid reeked of beer. It was obvious he had just come from that bar, Jacks.

He sat straight up when he saw Allie, startled. Then he began to laugh. "What is this—a bust?"

"Who is Arden Sellers?" Allie asked, almost menacing.

Trent Tucker's face clouded. "How do you know her?" he demanded, his voice every bit as forceful as Allie's.

"I don't know her. She's dead."

"What do you mean?"

"She had a rock climbing accident, on the cliffs. The Kingston cops found her body a few hours ago. There was a slip of paper on her with your name on it. I want to know how you knew her."

The young man was visibly shaken—stunned, as if he had been dealt a blow from a blunt object. He began to sway from his trunk as he attempted to stand. But he was too unsteady. Allie pushed him back down on the mattress.

"How did you know her?" Allie persisted.

"I met her in New York. We fell in love down there. She was coming to see me." He spoke the words mechanically.

"You were only in New York for one day," Allie reminded him. "How did all this happen?"

Trent Tucker didn't reply.

Allie walked out of the room. Mrs. Tunney was standing in the narrow hallway. "You better keep an eye on him," Allie cautioned.

"What did you do to him?" she asked bitterly.

"I did nothing."

Voegler walked on into the kitchen, where Charlie Gravis sat.

"Get me Didi's number where she's staying in New York," he ordered the older man.

"It's past midnight," Charlie protested.

"Just get me the number!"

Charlie went into the clinic office and returned with a small slip of paper. He handed it to Voegler.

Allie dialed. A woman answered, but it wasn't Didi. "Who's this?"

"Allie Voegler."

The female on the other end of the line seemed to know his name. She told him to hang on while she fetched Didi.

"I woke you, didn't I?"

"Yes, that you did. But who cares? It's good to hear from you, Allie. I've been thinking of you."

He gave a short, sarcastic laugh and then told Didi what he had learned from Chung and Trent Tucker's response to the news of the girl's death.

"You mean you're at my place now?"

"Yeah. Mrs. Tunney is with the kid."

"Stop calling him a kid. He's past twenty-one now."

"How about idiot instead of kid?"

"Why? Because he fell in love with a girl at

first sight? Do you know who Arden was? She was the bartender at Boots the night we were all there. He was probably calling her since he came home. No one knew about it."

There was a pause. Allie turned so that Charlie couldn't see or hear.

"When are you coming back?" he asked urgently.

"Soon, Allie, soon. But do me a favor. Have the Kingston police contact a Detective Phil Slater of the NYPD. He should know about the accident."

"Will do. I miss you, Dr. Nightingale. I'm so desperate to see you I even found Mrs. Tunney bearable."

He hung up and walked back to the room. Trent Tucker had his earphones back on. He was lying down, his eyes open. Mrs. Tunney sat quietly on the side of the bed.

The kid sensed his presence. He looked at Allie for a moment . . . a look of pain and hate.

Why do they always blame the messenger? Allie thought.

Six in the morning.

Didi sat alone in the living room. It was the first morning while staying at Ilona's that she had arisen at her regular hour. She looked down at the carpet. Should she do her usual yogic breathing exercises?

Her thoughts went to Trent Tucker and Arden Sellers. What a sad, sad twist. She knew that Detective Slater would be very suspicious. Was it another coincidence that Arden Sellers had decided to rock climb no more than a hundred yards from Carl Schirra's property? *At night?*

Hardly.

But it was that other "coincidence" that still rankled Didi: Tor and Darryl Yates together.

How odd it was. She had fixated on that one scene with Tor. Not the date. Not the ugly turn of events in his loft. Not the smashing of the art. Not her bad faith in going out with a man other than Allie. Even though, when she spoke to him on the phone, she could tell that Allie sensed something had happened.

She smiled. Should she make coffee? No, not yet. She folded her arms behind her head. The primal scene: Tor and Yates.

Didi remembered an undergraduate philosophy course. The professor had assigned a reading in Edmund Husserl, the founder of the philosophy called phenomenology.

No one in the class had understood the reading.

The prof told the class to shut their eyes and keep them shut until he said to open them.

There was laughter, but everyone complied.

They kept them shut for about thirty seconds; then the professor told them to open them.

"What you saw when you first opened your eyes just now—the colors, shapes, textures—is true. That first sudden glimpse before you had time to think, before anything mediated what you saw. That is what Husserl begins with . . . and ultimately ends with."

Yes. Didi had always remembered that little classroom game.

But this was the first time she had ever experienced any practical application of it to her life. It was as though her eyes had been closed; and now she had opened them. And what she saw was Torvald and Yates. That was a truth. And she'd be damned if it was a "coincidental" truth—no matter what Detective Slater said.

What other truths did he possess? Who else did he know?

I am going to find out, she thought. Then

she caught herself. A search for justice for a dead man she hadn't known? Or a refusal to relinquish an obsession?

As her old vet school professor Hiram Bechtold used to say: It really doesn't matter what cures the cow. Neither the cow nor the farmer cares.

Didi went into her valise and got a street map of Manhattan, which she had purchased some time ago but not yet used. She wrote another note to Ilona, saying this time that she was going out for a long walk to explore the city, and she'd be in the clinic by early afternoon. Then she put on her walking shoes and left the apartment.

Once on the street she consulted her map, identified a route that appeared to be "as the crow flies," and started off for the point of her surveillance mission.

She walked south on First Avenue, past the huge Bellevue Hospital complex, and turned west on Twenty-third Street. She then turned south on Fifth Avenue—all the way down to Washington Square Park. It was a beautiful summer morning, so she lingered just a moment there. After all, when she was a teenager this was one of the places she had longed to visit but had never made it.

Then out the south end of the park, onto La Guardia Place. Then a few blocks to Houston, and east for a few blocks to Greene Street.

She was now, according to her map, only three or four blocks from her destination. There was a coffee shop at Houston and Greene. She bought a large container with a sipping lid and a piece of lemon poppy seed cake and set out on the last leg of her trip.

It was only 7:20 in the morning when she took her first sip of coffee on a loading platform across the street from Tor's building. The walk had been exhilarating. The city was much more peaceful and quiet than she had ever imagined it could be—almost gentle.

The cake was too sweet, but the coffee was about the best she had ever tasted. It straightened her spine and put sizzle into her walk.

When she finished the repast, she slid back into the shadow of the building and waited.

There was a great deal of traffic on Canal Street, but virtually none on Greene, and little the other way, on Grand.

Didi noticed that virtually all the buildings on the street had loading docks. Manufacturers? Wholesalers? What did it matter? It was obvious they no longer did business here. There were no trucks or workers in sight.

As she waited, she watched the foot traffic, which was sparse. And she studied her street map. A knot of nervousness was beginning to clench and unclench in her stomach. She felt isolated, watched. She felt that she stood out like a sore thumb. This wasn't Hillsbrook.

Torvald the sculptor emerged from his loft building at 8:15, alone. He was wearing a faded, tight black polo shirt and a pair of khaki shorts splattered with paint. The first thought Didi had upon seeing him was: What a handsome man he is. He has the build of an Olympic swimmer.

Tor walked north on Greene. Didi followed a half block behind, on the opposite side of the street. She was fascinated by the way he walked— a kind of "I don't give a damn" stride—like an immature breeding bull turned out among the cows for the first time.

He turned east on Houston, north on Broadway, east on 10th Street, and vanished into a gym on 4th Avenue.

Didi was confused. Who goes into a gym without a gym bag?

She was sweating. She walked into a post office and waited there, her eyes on the gym entrance. The building had large windows and powerful air-conditioning. She wondered if the postal workers often caught colds from spending the workday in those frigid, swirling blasts.

Tor came out in fifteen minutes. Not alone. Again he was with Darryl Yates. They walked uptown slowly. Didi continued to follow. She could tell they were having an animated conversation. They crossed 14th Street and entered Union Square Park. They sat on a bench together. Didi sat down on a patch of grass about fifty yards from them. Two Asian schoolgirls shared it with her. They were studying for an exam. Summer school is rough, Didi remembered.

The two men stood up, shook hands, and parted.

Tor started walking back downtown. Yates, wearing a blue shirt and dark tie and carrying a manila folder, walked east out of the park.

She did not know what to do. She made a snap decision: follow Yates, not Torvald.

And follow him she did. He walked leisurely all the way to First Avenue—four long avenue blocks—and then headed up-town.

In twenty minutes Didi was once again passing Ilona's high-rise. It was ridiculous: She had made a complete circle.

At 37th Street and First Avenue, Yates climbed a set of stone steps and went into a gourmet shop, emerging with a bottle of mineral water. He sat down at one of the outdoor tables provided by the store and drank his water.

She waited by a large, gurgling fountain, obscured from Yates's view by the spray. In a while she saw a heavyset woman coming south on First. The woman climbed the steps and headed purposefully for Yates's table.

Once the woman was seated at the table, Didi peered through the foamy spray. How astonishing—she knew who the woman was. Her name was Janice. One of the Mazzini sisters. They too had been in the audience that night at Boots. Didi recalled that the sisters both worked at the United Nations. That was only a few blocks north.

What was going on? Some strange kind of support group? Didi had read about a terrible shooting on the Long Island Railroad a few years back. A crazed gunman had started firing in a commuter rail car. Many people were killed. The survivors, traumatized, sought solace in one another's company. Total strangers very quickly became intimate friends. Was this the kind of thing taking place among the witnesses to the Schirra murder?

The two people at the table settled in. It looked as if it was going to be a long siege. Didi's feet had begun to ache. Her back, too. She stank from sweat. And she was only two blocks from Ilona's.

So she ended her surveillance.

She walked quickly back to the apartment, showered, and changed.

Ilona was there to greet her when she entered the clinic. "Good news, Nightingale!" she announced excitedly. "The lab reports were negative. It isn't FIA."

"What is it then?" she asked, not really able to concentrate on Sweet William's problem.

"My hunch is that it might simply be a fatty acid deficiency. You know they require a lot more than dogs, and are usually given much less."

"Sounds good to me."

"What about Nightingale?" Ilona asked brightly. "Where did you wander today?"

Didi lied effortlessly. "I ended up in the Central Park Zoo. I wanted to see how those neurotic polar bears responded to the shirred puffin eggs you recommended for them."

"I never recommended any such thing. So, Nightingale, you're starting to make fun of me because of my peculiar hobby. You're saying to yourself, 'Poor Ilona is doing so well, but she's going to end up stranded on an ice floe somewhere in the Antarctic, all because she wanted to catch a glimpse of a bearded seal.' I know what you're thinking, Nightingale."

Didi smiled and patted her friend's arm. "Actually, I think it's in the grand tradition of lunatic veterinarians. Remember Tillotson?"

Ilona shook her head. "No. Who's she?"

"He," Didi corrected. "He was a famous racetrack vet who gave a few lectures during our junior year. I went to all of them. Anyway, it turned out that Tillotson's passion was collecting old hubcaps."

"Go figure," Ilona said.

That, indeed, was what Didi was doing.

* * *

The Kingston police department was adamant; there was nothing—absolutely nothing—to lead them to believe that it was anything other than an unfortunate climbing accident. It happened all the time—particularly to young people and particularly when they climbed "easy" cliffs during inclement weather or at night. They tended to be overconfident, and they slipped or twisted an ankle, or a sudden gust of wind spun them around. No, this young woman from Manhattan, Arden Sellers, simply fell and broke her neck.

That's what Detective Phil Slater was recounting to his partner, Follette, as they entered Arden Sellers's apartment over the laundromat on 8th Avenue between 17th and 18th Streets.

The superintendent, a Dominican, had let them in unhappily. "She was the best tenant here," he said. Then he made a gesture, rubbing his fingers together, to denote the fact that she tipped generously.

The apartment was cluttered. "Do you believe it?" Follette asked.

"You mean, do I believe it was an accident? I don't know what to believe."

The floor had obviously been subdivided because everything in the apartment, architecturally, was skewed. The single room that basically comprised the apartment was a simple rectangle—very small. But the apartment had a sizable walk-in kitchen and a very large bathroom.

The apartment seemed to have been used as an adjunct to Boots. Along one wall was stacked files of publicity photos, flyers, and other documents concerning performers at Boots. And there were many blank contracts.

There was much to do. And they were determined to do it carefully. Both detectives removed their jackets and hung them over chairs. Arden had obviously been a pathological magazine reader, because while there were few books in the room, magazines were all over—on shelves, on the floor, on the windowsills.

There was no bed in the room. She had obviously slept on the sofa. Follette checked it out. It did not open.

The clothes closet, only one, was sparse. Arden seemed to have had little interest in clothes. There were, however, many brushes and combs stacked on the shelf in the closet, so many that she might have been a collector.

There was a window fan as well as a floor fan in the apartment. Follette switched them both on.

"Shake out each magazine," Phil Slater ordered, and they both went to work, flinging the journals into one pile after examining each. There was no writing desk or any kind of file in the apartment, but there were several legal-size envelopes stacked on one side of the sofa, almost high enough to function as a coffee table.

Slater went through the envelopes one by one. He found personal papers—passport, birth certificate. He found old letters and photos. He found three term papers Arden had done several years ago at the University of Vermont. He found three old wedding rings in a stiff envelope. Her mother's, perhaps. And her grandmothers'? It appeared from the photographs that she came from a large family.

Follette found her bank statements on the kitchen counter. She had banked at Chemical. The most recent statement gave her balance as $106.

Then he went through all the drawers in the

kitchen cabinets. She must have been a serious cook; there were assorted whisks and eggbeaters. Then he found recipes—hundreds of them—torn out of magazines and newspapers and saved.

But it was the broom closet that yielded the real prize.

The packet was visible, resting on a collection of laundered and folded rags. It had a plastic cover. Follette pulled it down, scanned it briefly through the plastic, and called out, "More maps, Phil."

Slater came into the kitchen. They spread the maps on the table. The two men marveled in silence. It was a duplicate set of the maps they had found on the houseboat—the exact same counties.

Slater opened one of the maps. "Wait," he said. "These are a bit different. Look. They're marked."

Indeed, they were, but the marks were not intelligible. Simply red Magic Marker dots highlighting certain geographical areas.

The detectives opened all the maps full out. The most heavily marked map was for Dutchess County. The southwest corner had dozens of red dots around the towns and villages called Wappingers Falls, Hopewell Junction, Beacon, and Fishkill.

"That vet comes from around here, doesn't she?" Slater asked, tapping the map with his pencil.

"I think so."

"Maybe she knows what this all means."

Slater went to the phone and called his office. A civilian employee got Ilona Baer's number off Slater's Rolodex and read it back to him. He hung up and made the call. Ilona picked up. She put Didi on. Yes, Didi said, she would be happy to come over. When? Now. Fine.

Dr. Deirdre Quinn Nightingale showed up in exactly nineteen minutes. There were no preliminaries. Except for Follette smiling a bit lasciviously and Slater grunting.

Didi studied the maps in the kitchen. "Yes," she said, "I know all these towns quite well."

"What do the marks mean?" Slater asked.

"I don't know."

"Can you tell from the location what they signify? I mean, is it possible she is putting a dot next to each shopping center in the area?"

"Why shopping centers?" Follette interjected. "Why not banks? Or schools?"

"I have no idea what those marks mean," Didi said. "None at all."

Slater was distressed. He had been counting on her. He went to the sink and ran the water. Then he washed his face and drank from the faucet.

"Look," he said to Didi, turning swiftly. "What if I asked you to do us a very big favor?"

"Ask."

"How about going up there for us? You know the area. Just check out what the dots mean, what they stand for."

Didi thought about it. Why shouldn't I help them? I already am.

"I can get up there tomorrow," she said.

"Wonderful! Great! Thank you. The NYPD is forever in your debt. I will get the mayor to issue a special medal. I will—" And then Slater caught himself. Whew. The heat was getting to him.

"One thing. One thing," he said in what was now a more measured tone.

"What's that?" Didi asked.

"We have to make a stop at the houseboat. I want to make sure the maps are identical before you go riding around up there."

"Smart move," Follette agreed. "Everything's getting fuzzy."

"We'll go in a few minutes. Let's just finish up here."

"May I look around while you're finishing up?" Didi asked.

"Help yourself," said Slater.

Didi realized that she hadn't told Slater about the meeting between Yates and Mazzini that she had witnessed. She had no desire to do so; he would just bring up that word again—*coincidence*. Or maybe he would substitute *trivial*.

She walked slowly around the perimeter of the apartment, marveling at the junk a young woman could collect.

Then she saw the pile—the very high pile—of Boots circulars. It would be nice, she thought, to get the one that announced Abigail's appearance. No flyer had been posted inside or outside the club on the night of her debut—only that hand-lettered piece of paper announcing the Bayou Blasters—but that could have just been an oversight.

She knelt down beside the pile and began to look through the announcements. They were simple, basic—all the singers and musicians on a given evening listed according to time slot: 7 P.M., 9 P.M., 11 P.M., 1 A.M. Or 8 P.M., 10 P.M., midnight.

Once in a while there was a blurb about the singer or the band—things on the order of "Brilliant"—*Arkansas Gazette*. Country/Western singers for the most part. Most of them Didi had heard at one time or another on the radio or on the juke box at the cafe or one of the bars in Hillsbrook. As for the zydeco bands, although Didi knew little about that kind of music herself, she recognized some of the crazy names from her friend Rose's collection of cassettes.

No, there was no circular for that terrible night. Nothing to bring back to Abigail as a souvenir. Didi stood up and looked down at her hands, which had become a bit dusty from the papers. She went into the kitchen and washed up.

One thing was odd about those flyers, she realized as she turned her hands under the running water. There were very few 7 P.M. shows, perhaps one a month. Usually the entertainment started at eight or nine. And when there was a seven o'clock show, the performer was always a total unknown—like Abigail.

Didi thought about how the bad luck that persistently followed poor Abigail had definitely popped up here again. If she had been booked to perform on a night without a 7 P.M. show, she would never have witnessed that murder. there would only have been Abigail's debut. And what a wonderful thing that could have been.

"Ready?" Slater asked. He had found the key to the houseboat. He held it up, one of many on a ring, and jiggled it triumphantly.

The pigs were Charlie Gravis's responsibility. Dr. Nightingale was unhappy about his raising pigs on the place. The others were unhappy, too. But they ate the pork when it was dressed. They were hypocrites. At least the boss was consistent. She wouldn't touch it. Charlie knew, however, that she understood that the Spotted Poland China hogs he kept and fed and occasionally slaughtered had to do with his own sense of worth. He was a damn farmer, after all. Or at least he had been once upon a time. He wasn't a sponger.

After he cleaned Sara's pen, Charlie walked out of the barn and rested. It was a brilliant summer day. The sky was bereft of a single cloud. The sun was fierce. But the air was so dry the heat seemed irrelevant. It was so hot and dry that one sweated in cold beads.

A movement in the field caught his eye, on the far side of the field where it bordered the pine forest. The field itself had not seen alfalfa in many a year and was now a riot of dandelions and sunflowers.

It was Abigail out there. She was standing alone—in one of her strange poses, as if she were communing with someone or something.

Now, he thought, was as good a time as any to talk to her. In fact, it was the ideal time. The conversation had to be private.

He trudged out onto the field. Abigail didn't hear him until he was about twenty feet away. Then she turned slowly and, seeing it was him, smiled and gave one of her funny, endearing little half waves.

"There's a family of rabbits out here," she said, delighted.

"That's nice," Charlie replied. He was breathing a bit heavily.

"And there's a fox in the woods, Charlie!"

"I would imagine there are many, Abby."

She nodded, affirming Charlie's comment.

They stood in silence a while. There was a

great deal of rustling beneath and around them. It could be woodchucks, Charlie thought. Or maybe those rabbits. It might be just about anything.

"Are you still sad about what happened in New York City, Abigail?"

"Yes. No one deserves to die like that."

"No, I don't mean that. I mean about you not getting a chance at a singing career."

"Oh, that. Maybe. I don't know, Charlie. I don't really think about it much."

Charlie wondered what she really did think about. All he said was, "You have a beautiful voice, Abigail. One day a lot of people are gonna find that out."

She smiled thanks at him.

"Maybe not just people," Charlie added.

She did not understand what he meant. She tilted her head, giving him a quizzical look.

"What I'm saying is, it's not only people who like . . . need music. Don't you remember what happened during that storm, Abby?"

"What storm, Charlie?"

"Just a few days ago. A morning storm. Promise Me was going crazy cause of the lightning and thunder, and you went into the barn and sang for him."

"Oh, yes."

"That was a beautiful rendition of that song."

"Thank you."

"Specially the way you kept doing that one line . . . Let my people go."

Abigail hummed a bit of the hymn.

"Yes, that's it. Yeah. Everybody needs a little music to make them happy. People. Horses. Even the cows. Did you know that, Abigail?"

"Did you say *cows*, Charlie?"

"That's right. You didn't realize they like music, too, did you?"

"No, Charlie, I didn't."

"Most certainly cows need their music."

There was a long silence. Abigail seemed to be listening for the rabbit family.

"Would you sing for some cows as a favor to me, Abby?" he blurted out.

"But we don't have any cows, Charlie."

"What about someone else's cows?"

"Are you making a joke, Charlie?"

"Abigail, I am more serious than I have ever been in my life." A yellowjacket buzzed Charlie's nose just then. He brushed it away. "I want you, as a favor to me, to make a tape recording of that song—just the way you sang it to quiet the horse the other day. Think you could do that for me?"

"Sure I will. But are you really going to play it for cows?"

"One cow. Ten cows. A hundred. One day, even a million of them. We're going to enter a land of milk and honey, honey."

He felt like grabbing Abigail's hands and dancing around the field with her, the two of them like crazed rabbits.

Slater started to insert the key into the lock of the houseboat door. It was immediately apparent there was no need for a key. The door was open.

"Trouble," he growled. He stepped back and firmly pushed Didi to one side. He gestured to Follette, who already had his weapon drawn.

They could hear nothing inside. But there was traffic on the Hudson, and it would be hard to hear anything going on in the house boat.

Slater took a big breath. He drew his weapon and slowly turned the knob. Then, flinging the door open, he and Follette rushed inside.

No one there. Everything the same. Nothing touched since their last trip out.

But five minutes later they knew that the packet of maps and the rope ladder were gone.

Slater sat down heavily on the bottom of the bunk bed. "She took them. She came here and took them. She used the rope ladder to climb with and it killed her. And she took the maps. Why? Because they're important. And she had the master set, so these could be destroyed. She thought sooner or later we would find out what the maps were about. She had to get rid of Schirra's set."

"We don't know that for sure," Follette noted.

"Then who took it? Snow White?" Slater retorted loudly. He dug into his pocket and pulled out the packet of maps found in Arden's apartment—what he had called the master set. He stripped the Dutchess County map from the pack and handed it to Didi.

"You're still game?" he asked.

"Yes," she said, taking the map. It was so light in her hand, so light.

"You'll do a good job, won't you? It's important."

"I'll do the best I can."

Didi was already thinking of the mechanics of the operation. She didn't want to do it alone. Rose Vigdor would come with her if Didi asked her. Yes, that would be best. When she got back to Ilona's apartment, she would phone home. Rose didn't have a telephone. Didi would tell Trent Tucker to bring Rose back to the house and have her call Ilona's place. Didi would tell Rose what was happening. Trent could drive Rose the following morning to the huge new shopping mall near Wappingers Falls and drop her there. Didi would rent a car in Manhattan, drive up, meet up with Rose, and the two would follow the map together. Yes, it was a good working plan. As for her dogs, Trent Tucker would take care of them. He had done it before.

"I would never live in a place like this," Follette said.

"And I would never climb a Hudson River cliff," Slater replied. "So what?"

Charlie had the back of Mother's General Store all to himself. He sat down on a chair with his German beer and an envelope and pencil. The envelope came from an old electric bill. He wet the tip of the pencil and readied himself to make history with his words.

The headline for the ad, he had already figured out. He wrote:

DAIRY FARMERS! ARE YOU CAUGHT IN THE SQUEEZE?

He just loved that headline. The "squeeze," of course, was the eternal one that had bankrupted him and about a million other farmers. Milk prices kept falling. Feed prices kept rising. And the milk yield remained the same. Unless, of course, you could raise the money to expand. But the loans had dried up. Yep. A squeeze was a squeeze. And this one never stopped.

Now for the rest of the ad. He had to come up with something brief and yet strong. He had three hours to do it. If he could phone it in within three hours, it would appear in four local weeklies tomorrow morning. Thousands of dairy farmers in a three-county area would read it. Well, he thought, maybe dairy farmers don't read so much. Anyway, hundreds of them would read it.

He put pen to paper . . . or, as it was, stubby pencil to crinkled envelope.

I CAN INCREASE MILK YIELD BY 20 PERCENT.
NO DRUGS. NO HORMONES. *INEXPENSIVE. SAFE.*
GUARANTEED TO WORK.

He stopped writing and took a long swig of the beer. Damn, this German stuff was good. It had a kind of sweet bite. He looked at the label. Oh. Czech, not German.

Then he read over what he had written after the headline. Pretty good. He liked it. Kind of mellow, but dramatic. He needed one or two more lines to put the finishing touch on things. Something that would pack a punch.

I may have to stretch the truth, he thought . . . a bit . . . an eenie meenie little bit. After all, this whole thing was about economic survival. His. Or rather, economic renewal. He was down so low he couldn't get any lower.

So he wrote:

You heard about the Gravis Method.
You read about it.
Now put it to work for you.

Charlie loved it, but he did study it carefully. How much of a lie was it? Well, there had been experiments in the 60s and 70s. That was no lie. But nowhere had he read that these experiments were named after anyone in particular, let alone called the Gravis Method.

He debated the indiscretion. Well, it was *now* called the Gravis Method. He was the one who had rescued the system from obscurity. So why not?

He said to the envelope, "I'm going to just let you lie about for a bit." He folded the envelope, put it in his pocket, went into the store, bought another beer, and sat back down.

When he was halfway through the second bottle, he pulled the envelope out and perused it critically again. He liked it even more after the passage of time. He went directly to the pay phone at the foot of the porch.

Chapter 7

Didi saw her standing forlornly in front of an eyeglass store. She pulled the rented car right up to her, swung open the passenger door, and yelled out, "Need a lift, baby?"

A very happy Rose Vigdor climbed in. "It is so good to see you, Night Light. I mean, what's happened to us? Have we changed places or something? I thought I was the big city girl. You're supposed to be the bumpkin, and here you are driving upstate to take a poor little country girl for a ride. Life is getting so weird, Didi. And that whacked-out young man who works for you, Trent Tucker, he's so goddamn depressed he didn't say a word on the drive here."

Didi told her quickly about the death of Arden Sellers—and how Trent Tucker's name and phone number had been found on her body. Then she pulled out the map, opened it, and explained the task to Rose.

"Are we doing this for money?" Rose asked.

"Of course not," Didi replied brusquely.

"Don't get huffy, girlfriend. I mean, why not get paid for it? The NYPD hires vets to look after the police horses, don't they?"

"I suppose they do. But this is just a favor to a friend."

"Who?"

"Myself." She couldn't really give Rose a capsule synopsis of what had happened between her and Tor, and all the psychological ramifications of it.

"Let's go," Rose pleaded. "Get me out of this shopping center before I die."

Didi handed the map to her. "You navigate," she said. "Take me to the first dot south of Wappingers Falls. The detective in charge of the case wants that thick cluster covered first. One dot at a time."

"Do you have any idea what they mean?"

"Not the foggiest."

"What if they mean nothing? Just . . . well, just dots."

"We'll find out, won't we?"

Rose immediately began giving specific instructions. "Right here. Left here."

They reached the location of the first red dot in about eight minutes.

"I never saw such a detailed map. It gives you every street," Rose noted.

"Detective Slater told me it's the kind of map that salesmen use."

They sat in the car and looked around. It was one of those small rural dead ends. Two houses in sight, one on each corner; then empty, unweeded lots.

Then a tumbledown building.

"The dot, I assume, on the map, is right where that shell is."

They left the car and approached the tumbledown building. Only two walls were left, but they were stone. Behind the rubble was a small, untended cemetery consisting of eight or nine stones, several of which had fallen down. A wrought iron gate between the rubble and the cemetery plot was still standing.

"I've got news for you," Rose said. "This is a church."

"You mean because of the cemetery?"

"Yes. And because of *that*." She pointed to a still-standing gate. "Look closely."

Didi looked. There were letters worked into the gate, baroque but readable: WE PREACH CHRIST CRUCIFIED, RESURRECTED, AND COMING AGAIN.

"Are you sure we're on the dot?" Didi asked.

Rose thrust the map under her nose. "Right on the dot. Right smack on it."

They got back into the car.

"So what does it mean?" asked Rose.

"I don't know. Yet. Let's go to the next dot."

They reached the next dot in about four minutes. It was on a steep hill behind a large regional high school.

This dot also covered a church. It was a standing, operating church, white clapboard, like in New England. There was a larger cemetery in the back. There was a small steeple and a bell. It was quite charming. It was Congregational in persuasion.

"What is going on?" asked Didi.

"Maybe the people who made the dots were compiling a guidebook to the old churches of Dutchess County."

"Or maybe they were robbing graves," Didi noted.

"Yes. A vampire cult. All evidence seems to

point to that. The bodies were then shipped in ice-cream trucks downstate and sold in expensive restaurants. The—"

Rose was off on one of her imaginative tears. Didi had to interrupt. "Let's go to the next one."

They "visited" five more dots, the last one being very close to the Beacon/Newburgh bridge. All five were churches. Some were functioning, some boarded up, some ruined. But they were all churches with cemeteries.

"Do we keep going?" Rose asked.

"What's the point?" Didi asked.

They were sitting in the car. Didi switched the air-conditioning on. She felt very tired, very lonely.

"I'm going back," she finally said. "I arranged to meet Detective Slater at four o'clock in the Central Park Zoo. I'll tell him what I found and give him the map back."

"The zoo. Why the zoo?"

"Ilona is a nutritional consultant for the zoo. I lied to her the other day and told her I had gone to the zoo to check out her menus. Now I want to make good on the lie. Besides, the detective was amenable. He's a devotee of an old TV cop program called *Naked City*. He told me the cops on the show would often meet informants in the zoo. It's a safe place."

"So that's what you've become, Didi—a snitch."

"Hardly."

"Well, it was nice seeing you, Quinlan."

"Hey, listen, Rose. Why don't you come back to Manhattan with me."

"Now?"

"Yes. Right now. It's been a long time since you visited your old haunts. The scenes of the crimes, one could say."

"But I have no clothes with me, and no place to stay. I can't just go back with you now. But damn, yes, I would love to visit the city again. Nature Girl is getting thirsty for a whole lot of things." She laughed. "Like steam heat for the coming winter."

"You and Ilona are about the same size. If nothing of hers fits you, I have two working credit cards. And you'll stay with us. Ilona loves company. The more the merrier."

"But my dogs . . ."

"Trent Tucker is watching them. He'll keep on looking after them for a while longer."

"I don't know . . ."

But Didi could tell from the wistful expression in her friend's eyes that it was all settled. She felt relieved. She wanted her company.

There was plenty of time. They drove back leisurely to Manhattan, and Didi turned in the vehicle. Then the two friends went to the Central Park Zoo.

They wandered about a bit, spending an inordinate period of time with the polar bears. Then into the Jungle Habitat where Didi was surprised to discover that the tortoises were dwarfs compared to Krista Michaels's Gruesome.

Then to the Penguin House, where they were to meet Detective Slater. It was delightfully frigid in that place, and they sat on the bench across from the glass-enclosed living space of the penguins. The birds waddled along the ice, diving into the deep water that ran between ice and viewer's glass. It was like two distinct civilizations facing each other.

"Do you think they know they're in a zoo?" Rose asked.

"I don't know what they think."

"I don't understand why your friend Ilona would want to be a nutritional consultant for antarctic creatures. I mean, the menu must be sparse. I would like to be a consultant for the feeding of hyenas. I understand they're the most omnivorous creatures on earth. They will eat almost anything. Can you imagine the fun of planning their menus?"

Detective Slater arrived, stifling the hyena nutrition fantasy.

He sat down next to Didi. She introduced him to Rose. The two shook hands. Didi handed him the map and told him what she and Rose had found.

"Everywhere I go I am assailed by this air-conditioning," he noted, almost absentmindedly.

"This isn't air-conditioning," Rose said, "it's an old fashioned ice box."

"During heat waves it always get crowded," he added.

Then he began to curse violently under his breath, smacking the map again and again against one palm. "I was sure these marks were the key—the break in the case. You know what I mean. Churches? Cemeteries? Garbage in and garbage out."

He stared at the penguins as if seeing them for the first time, then suddenly burst into bitter laughter. "You know, I've worked all kinds of cases. Mob hits. Drug wars. Jealous wives blowing away husbands. Rich kids shooting their teachers. Homeless lunatics braining anybody who happens to be walking by with a flower in their lapel, because the loony's deathly afraid of carnations. All kinds of killings. But the ones I fear the most . . . the ones that really are like smashing your stupid head against a stone wall . . . are these middle-class murders. There are no drugs, no crazies, no Mafia dons. Just people trying to make a living and make it through the world day by day. Excuse me, I'm beginning to babble. But, do you know what I mean?"

Rose and Didi exchanged glances. "I think I understand," Didi said. Although she didn't really. "I'm sorry about the map," she added.

"Believe me, so am I. I would have bet a month's pay that the map was significant, that the dots meant something. It just figured. Arden Sellers took the maps out of the houseboat. Why? To remove evidence, obviously. Then she went upstate. Why? To destroy evidence in Schirra's cabin. I don't know what was there. Surely, not more maps. We searched the place, but there was nothing there. At least nothing we could find."

"She also took the rope ladder from the houseboat," Didi said.

"Yeah, she did. But so what? The young lady was a rock climber."

"But maybe the evidence to be destroyed was not in Schirra's cabin," Didi offered.

"What do you mean?"

"Maybe she wasn't climbing for fun. Maybe there was something in or on the cliffs near Schirra's place that she had to get to."

Slater laughed, a little derisively. "Yeah. And maybe she was searching for a miraculous bird's egg." He stood up, folded the map, and placed it in his jacket pocket. "I want to thank you very much," he said to Didi, then nodded to Rose. With that, he was gone.

"He walks like my Uncle Jack," Rose confided in a whisper. "Like a sailor—from side to side."

"I like him," Didi said.

"Me, too."

"He's sort of like an urban lawnmower."

"What a brilliant description, Dr. N."

"Glad you think so. Now, before I take you to Ilona's, I want you to take *me* to that fancy bar on Madison Avenue where you picked up that Frenchman."

"What Frenchman?"

"Rose, don't tell me you've forgotten. Since you moved up to Hillsbrook, I've heard that story at least twice a year."

"Calm down, girlfriend. Yes, I remember it. Are you sure you want to go there now?"

"Why not? We have time to kill. Or would you prefer to go rock climbing?"

Rose narrowed her eyes. When Dr. Nightingale put a touch of the bitters in her words, she was up to something.

"I didn't mention anything about rock climbing."

"No, you didn't. Sorry to snap at you, Rose."

"Sure, I'll take you to that bar. If I can remember where it is." Rose started to rise off the bench. Didi gently pulled her down.

"What is it?"

"Do you know anything about penguin stones, Rose?"

"No."

"Some kinds of penguins present small stones to the one they want to mate with. A gift. Or a bribe. Depending on how you look at it."

"Yeah. So?"

"Well, look at the penguins across the aisle.

If one of them lost a stone, where would he look?"

"In the water, I presume."

"Exactly."

"So?"

"So when rock climbers are looking for something they've lost, where do they look?"

"In the rocks?"

"Precisely."

"I thought it was your friend Ilona who was a specialist on penguins."

"Uh-uh. Actually her specialty is cats."

It was around midnight. Trent Tucker was seated in a booth at the bar called Jacks. His friend Legrand was across from him. Legrand had a job, so he was buying the beers.

Trent had just come from Rose Vigdor's place. He had fed all three of her dogs and taken them for a run.

"You know," he said dreamily to Legrand, "if I was going to kill myself, I wouldn't use a .357. I'd use one of those new .22-caliber pieces. I hear the real hit men use them. Maybe because it makes a small hole . . . no mess."

"Get hold of yourself, man," Legrand

warned. "Sure it's sad and all. But people die all the time. You didn't even know the girl."

"What do you mean, I didn't know her?"

"You said you met her *once*."

Trent Tucker bristled. "But she was coming up here to see me. I wrote her. She had my number on her when she died. She was coming to see *me*."

"So you say," the other man said cynically. Then he saw the fury in Trent's eyes, and he held up both his hands in a gesture of apology.

His anger past, Tucker leaned back in the booth and closed his eyes. "I want to be honest. It was more than just her, Legrand. You know what I'm saying. I thought I would go down there and stay with her. The city is great. I mean it's different. I like walking on the streets. I like the noise and the people. It ain't like up here. No one gives a damn what you do. Everybody goes to hell in their own way."

"You would have got tired of it. You would have come back. A lot do."

"And she was beautiful," Trent Tucker intoned, as though the other man had never spoken. "Really beautiful and different and she stood on her own damn feet and she seemed to run that whole place, but she was kind to me, and I knew she liked me, too, Legrand. I could tell from the way . . . well, you know what I mean. She looked at me like I was . . . ah hell . . . like an astronaut."

Legrand thought that very funny. He laughed. Trent Tucker opened his eyes, staring again.

They both heard the noise from the bar and looked over that way.

The bartender was gesticulating.

Legrand said, "You know what Charlie Gravis says about you?"

"What?"

"A boy like that needs a dairy herd to look after, or he gets in all kinds of trouble."

Trent smiled for the first time that evening. "You know what old Charlie can do with his cows and his wisdom." Then he gestured to the bartender that he couldn't hear or understand what the hell he was saying, given the volume of the jukebox.

The bartender made another gesture.

"He's saying there's a phone call for you," Legrand explained.

"Here? Don't be stupid. I'm not even supposed to be here. Nobody calls me here."

"Well, check it out. Maybe it's that cop. What's his name? Voller."

Trent Tucker knew that he meant Allie Voegler. He walked over to the bar and accepted the receiver from the bartender.

"Yes? Who is this?"

"It's Didi Nightingale," the voice at the other end said.

Tucker was speechless. What the hell was she doing, calling him at Jacks? And why was she using that name with him—Didi? He called her Miss Quinn, like all the others who worked at the house, or he called her Dr. Nightingale, but never by her first name—not to her face at least. After all, she was the boss.

"How are you feeling?" Didi asked.

It took a minute for him to answer. "So-so," he said warily.

"I need a favor."

Again, he was stunned. This was the boss, for God's sake. He lived in the house that she owned. She didn't ask "favors." She told them all what to do.

"Sure, Miss Quinn."

"Who's there with you?"

"My friend Legrand."

"Good. He can help."

"Help with what?"

"That girl who died—that girl you liked—Arden Sellers . . ."

"Yeah?"

She didn't die climbing for fun, Trent. She was trying to get something."

"Like what?"

"I don't really know. But it was up there, on those cliffs. Do you know where she was climbing, Trent? Just south of the Kingston Bridge. The man who was shot to death in that bar in New York had a place nearby. Just between that nursing home and the bridge. That's where she was climbing. Do you know the area?"

"Like the back of my hand," he said. As a kid, he and his friends had literally lived along the cliffs, bicycling there, camping, getting into all kinds of mischief.

"Then you know which path she would have taken up the cliffs."

"There ain't . . . aren't . . . any paths. Just cliffs that are sheer and cliffs with crumbly outcroppings. It's the climbers who make the paths, and then the rocks just seem to tumble back into place. It's not hard climbing there."

"Go up there for me, Trent. See if you can find what she was looking for."

"Go up there? When?"

"Now. Right now. Take your friend with you."

"I don't know, Miss Quinn . . ." He looked at his friend in the booth. Legrand saluted him with his beer bottle.

"What am I supposed to be looking for?" Tucker asked then. "What kind of thing was it she was trying to find?"

"I don't know," Didi had to admit. She laughed nervously. "But I think it's smaller than a bread box." That was an expression her mother had used habitually—bigger or smaller than a bread box. She had never quite known where it came from, but people seemed to understand it immediately.

"There are hundreds of places you could hide stuff on those cliffs, Miss Quinn. All kinds of places. Ledges. Tunnels. Rat holes. Squirrel nests."

"I understand what you're saying, Trent. But I need you to try, anyway. Just be careful. I imagine you'll first have to locate the path she took from below. Do you have a good flash?"

"Yeah. In the pickup."

"Do you know how to reach me at Ilona Baer's?"

"Who?"

"The friend I'm staying with in Manhattan. Take down the phone number."

She gave him the phone number. Tucker scrawled it on a bar napkin.

"Call me the minute you get back. No matter what time it is. Just call me at that number. I'll be waiting. Okay?"

Trent Tucker stared at the receiver. He finally understood that a silent message was also being transmitted. Dr. Nightingale was saying that the young woman he had so wildly desired was implicated in the violent death of the nightclub owner.

"Okay. I'll give it a shot," he said.

Didi hung up and walked quietly to the door. She opened it and peered into the living room. Rose was fast asleep on the plush sectional. Didi could see that the light under Ilona's bedroom door had gone out. She too was sleeping. The living room was bathed with moonlight pouring through the windows.

She tiptoed into the living room and over to the bookcase. It was going to be a long night waiting, and she needed something to read. Her eyes scanned the volumes on the shelves. *Diseases and Surgery of the Cat.* No. *The Lame Horse.* She smiled. Did Ilona treat Central Park carriage horses, too? A monograph entitled "Social Behavior of Kittens." No. Another monograph on bacterial meningitis. No.

She moved on to the shelf devoted to Ilona's passion—frigid zones. She selected an old paperback, *My Life with the Eskimo*, written by a Scandinavian with an unpronounceable name.

Then she went into the kitchen, stole four Milano cookies and half a glass of 2 percent milk. She returned to her room, shutting the door softly behind her. For just a moment, for just a brief moment, she felt Allie Voegler's presence. And she felt sad.

The Eskimo book kept her awake for two hours. She was fascinated by the author's attempt to avoid sexual specifics in Eskimo life. What happens when five naked hunter-gatherers sleep in an igloo warmed by a seal blubber lamp and outside is a howling, shifting sea of ice? Things must happen.

Didi fell asleep just past two. At three she woke, finished the cookies, and waited. The phone did not ring.

She dozed off at three-thirty.

Then the phone jangled in her ear. She woke quickly and made a desperate grab at the receiver, snatching it up even before the first ring was finished.

It was Trent Tucker.

"Where are you calling from?" she asked in a hushed voice.

"Legrand's house."

"Good. What happened?"

He talked fast, excitedly, triumphantly. "I found a whole lot of stuff. The place was marked. It was easy as hell to find. Ribbons on spikes only about ten yards from the top of the cliff. And then a hole dug right into the gravel and dirt. Deep. Like a rabbit hole."

"And what did you find?"

"First some clothes, wrapped up real tight—two lined vests, sheepskin lined. And then two small wire cutters. They looked like wire cutters anyway. And a pair of thick gloves."

"Anything else?"

"Two baggies."

"What do you mean by 'baggies'?"

"You know. Those clear plastic bags you keep food in."

"Was there anything in them?"

"Yeah. There was a bankbook in one—a savings bankbook. From a Columbia County bank. There was . . ."

"What? What? Go on."

"There's a balance of $106,000 showing."

"Whose name is on it?"

"Carl Schirra. But the money's in trust for Arden Sellers."

Didi felt the back of her neck begin to sweat. "And in the other bag?"

"Paper. It's an application form. All folded up."

"Application for what?"

"To register a trademark with the U.S. Patent Office."

"Filled out?"

"No. It's blank. But somebody wrote something on the side of it—in ink."

"What does it say?"

"Hudson Blue."

"That's all?"

"That's all. Just 'Hudson Blue.' "

"You've done an incredible job, Trent. Are you okay?"

"It was a piece of cake."

"All right. Now listen carefully. The first thing in the morning, I want you to go into town and photocopy the first two pages of that bankbook. And then the application. Then go to the post office and mail the original bankbook and the original application Express Mail to this place . . . Wait."

She gave him Phil Slater's precinct address.

"What about the other stuff?" Trent asked.

"Just hold on to it. Now listen. After you mail the items, take the Xerox copies and fax them to me from my office in the clinic. You'll find Ilona Baer's fax number on the side of the machine with a whole bunch of other numbers."

"But I don't know how to fax."

"Ask Abigail. She'll show you. Or Charlie will."

"Okay."

"Everything clear?"

"Yeah."

"Thank you," Didi said and hung up.

She felt elated, confused, and exhausted all at the same time. What the hell did Hudson Blue mean?

She dialed Phil Slater's number and told his answering machine the basics. Who had found what and where. That the items were being sent to him Express Mail. That the money in

Schirra's savings bankbook was in trust for Aden Sellers. That the blank application for a registered trademark had the words Hudson Blue scribbled on it.

She hung up and fell asleep.

"Pick it up! Pick it up!"

The words woke her. She sat up violently, confused. She could see Ilona in the living room, pointing. And behind her, Rose, staring out the window with a big smile and a big mug of coffee in her hand.

Dazed, Didi realized the phone was ringing.

She picked it up.

"This is Phil Slater," a quiet voice said. Not his usual gruff voice.

"For me?" Ilona shouted.

Didi pointed to herself.

"Did you get my message?" she asked.

There was silence. Then he exploded over the phone. "Who the hell do you think you are? What gives you the right to authorize something like this? Who the hell do you think you are? A lieutenant in the NYPD? You don't just send kids up on dangerous climbs because you have a goddamn hunch. Are you some kind of nut?"

And he babbled on a bit more. Didi said not a word. Nor did she hang up. She just waited.

There was another long silence. Then Slater said, "I don't know what it means, but they're the first pieces of hard evidence we got. The first things you can sink your teeth into."

"Glad to be of service," she said archly.

The phone clicked off.

"Breakfast!" Ilona shouted.

Chapter 8

"Remember, Charlie!" Ike Badian said, shifting gears as they encountered the first steep hill of Route 28 west of Kingston.

"Remember what?"

"I want no part of your schemes. I'm just coming along because you asked me . . . because you said you need a real working farmer as a front. I'm doing it because you're an old friend, but I don't like it one bit."

Charlie just nodded. He was thinking of this Roy Brixton, who was the most promising of the dairy farmers who had answered his ad by telephone. That's where they were headed: to Brixton's dairy operation in Delaware County.

"And I'm not telling any lies to make you look good," Ike Badian added.

"Anything you say," Charlie answered. He

felt potent, sure of himself, on the brink of a success beyond even his wildest dreams.

They reached the Brixton Place in forty minutes. It was just inside the Delaware County line.

Roy Brixton was much younger than Charlie had imagined he would be—about forty—a big man wearing rubberized "mucking out" pants even in the August heat.

He led Charlie and Ike into the kitchen of his house by the backdoor. There was evidence of a wife and children, but no one was present in person. He brought out cans of beer and some cheese.

"Now give me the details," Brixton said, turning one of the chairs around and straddling it.

"Like the ad said. We've found a safe way to increase yield. We aim for a twenty percent increase the first week."

"The first week?" Brixton was impressed.

"That's right. It costs you fifty dollars up front, as a consulting fee. You don't pay a cent more unless there's a charted twenty percent increase in the first week. And then you pay twenty dollars a week for the installed system . . . as long as you want. In essence, you are renting it. Twenty a week for a twenty percent increase in milk. You can't beat that."

"You're talking herd yield, aren't you?" Brixton asked.

"Right. It don't work all the time for all cows. But it works on the statistical group," Charlie retorted, though he really hadn't the slightest idea what he was saying. A vision was coming to him. A thousand farmers paying twenty bucks a week in perpetuity. He couldn't even imagine how much he would pocket.

"And how do you do this?"

"Well, it's based on a method that was developed at the University of Iowa and Penn State a few years back."

"But what is it? Do you really install something in the barn? Do you add something to the feed?"

"No. It's music."

"Music? Are you serious?"

"A special kind of music. Singing."

Roy Brixton sat back precariously on the straddled chair. He ran his thick fingers through his hair. He had an incredulous look on his sun-burnt face.

"You two dairy farmers?" he asked.

"Sure are," Charlie said.

Brixton laughed. "Hell, I'll try anything once."

He left the kitchen and came back a minute later with a checkbook. "Who do I make the check out to?"

"Charles M. Gravis."

He filled in the name and amount and handed the check to Charlie.

"So when does it start?"

"Tomorrow night probably. The system goes from dusk to dawn. But I need a look at your barn now."

Brixton led them out of the house and to the barn. It was one of those large, new, multipurpose structures.

Twenty-eight milk cows at the north end. Feed and machinery in the center. Hogs on the other end. It was beautiful.

As Charlie and Ike walked back to the vehicle, Charlie said, "You stick with me and you'll be a rich man."

It was all Ike Badian could do to keep a straight face.

It was late in the afternoon. The air conditioner had been turned down a bit. There was a tray of goodies on the coffee table—and bottles of chilled wine—and a bottle of good champagne—and lace napkins.

Ilona Baer was throwing an impromptu party for her two houseguests.

"Sort of like we were back in school, isn't it? Without the poverty, of course," she said. "Afternoon relaxation. My, I've always loved afternoons, whether there was a man around or not."

Didi was quiet. Ilona and Rose alternated speaking, almost like an operatic duo. And the more they drank, the closer became their collaboration, voice-wise, that is.

Ilona talked about how she loved treating cats because they were so quirky. What seemed to be the case never was.

Then Rose talked about a bar she used to go to in the West Village and the men she met there and the times she had. Funny times. Pathetic times.

Then Ilona talked about the Antarctic. And "umiaking" in the Arctic . . . someplace like the Bay of Alaska. Didi knew the umiak was an Eskimo whaling boat. She had read it only the night before when she was waiting for Trent Tucker's call. That was about all she knew.

Rose talked about a young waiter who once fell in love with her while she was at the Westbury Hotel, attending a cocktail party for a British fashion photographer. The young man turned out to be an actor, of course. And so the affair ended quickly.

Didi was listening, but not very carefully. Her mind was on the dead man and the dead girl. No matter how many times during the day she had intellectually grappled with the bankbook and the trademark application and the scribbled words *Hudson Blue,* they did not reveal a bloody thing to her except that Schirra and Sellers were obviously lovers—or at least closely connected in some way over and above being co-workers at Boots. Yet, the facts didn't seem truly relevant. They were like the dots on the map marking churches and cemeteries.

What did seem relevant began to loom larger and larger in her head.

Tor. Tor above all. And the fact that he had met with Yates. Yates, and the fact that he had met with Mazzini. And then there was that peculiar, nagging fact of the seven o'clock performance once a month at Boots. Only once a month, usually on a Wednesday or Thursday. The performer always a newcomer.

The more wine she drank, the more her friends babbled on, the more these facts obsessed her.

She remembered what she had thought on her stakeout of Darryl Yates—that maybe all these mysterious meetings among the eyewitnesses—supposedly strangers to one another—were part of a kind of support group, meant to ease one another's pain.

"What's the matter with you, girl? Why are you so quiet?"

Didi looked up. "I'm thinking, Rose."

"That's unhealthy in the afternoon," said Ilona.

"If you're in a club of fools, you'd better act like one," Rose noted, taking a healthy swig from her wineglass.

"I certainly am a fool," admitted a now tipsy Ilona.

Didi felt a chill. Had Rose put her finger on it? Not random strangers walking into a club to hear a young singer. But some kind of club . . . some kind of group . . . a *meeting*.

"I want to hear Rosie's story about the Frenchman again," Didi said.

Ilona applauded. Soon Rose was in the middle of the tale. Didi excused herself from the room.

She walked into the bedroom, shut the door, and dialed Phil Slater's number.

He answered gruffly. "Got something for me?" he asked.

"I think so."

"What is it?"

"Did you ever uncover any connection between the eyewitnesses?"

"What do you mean by 'connection'?"

"Did they know each other?"

"Of course not. But you tell me. You and your friends were also witnesses. Did *you* have a connection with the others—or they with you? What the hell are you talking about anyway? Did they know each other before the shooting? The answer is no."

"But how do you know that? How can you be so sure?"

"They were all interviewed. Just like you and your friends were interviewed. No one said anything about being acquainted with anyone else there. They all said the same thing: that they had just walked in. Except for you and your people, of course. You were there to hear the girl sing."

"Detective Slater," Didi said quietly, "I have good reason to believe that Darryl Yates knew the Mazzini sisters before the shooting." She was stretching the truth a bit.

Slater fell silent for a long time. Didi knew she had struck a nerve.

Slater finally spoke again. "They all said the same thing . . . didn't they? 'I just came in to hear some music.' "

"Right," confirmed Didi, her voice heavy with sarcasm. "All that unanimity."

It was as if she could hear the detective thinking.

"You know, Detective, sometimes I look at a cow with a bad hind leg. It seems to bother her. She is favoring it. Now, the farmer thinks she stumbled in pasture. My assistant thinks she was kicked. But I'm always suspicious. Because things are never what they seem. It could well be an esophageal obstruction. Symptoms often pop up in the strangest places, and they often hide the real disorder. You follow that, don't you?"

"I'll get on this now," Phil Slater said, and hung up immediately.

Didi went back into the living room to join the other two women. She was able to catch the tail end of the French waiter story. Ilona was laughing uncontrollably. Then the phone rang again.

Ilona took the call on the kitchen extension. Didi and Rose did not speak, boldly listening in on Ilona's conversation. Except Ilona wasn't talking, only listening. In a few minutes she came back into the room.

"That was Krista Michaels. Sweet William is recovering just fine. All that juicy animal gristle and muscle is making him a happy thug again."

Didi shot out of her seat suddenly. "Oh, my God!" she cried.

"What's the matter?" the others said in unison.

"When you said that Sweet William was recovering, I suddenly remembered Molson. He was also recovering."

"Molson?" Rose asked. "Who is Molson?"

"The cat in Boots. He jumped up on Mrs. Tunney that night. But the club is now shut tight. There is no more Boots. And there's no food or water there."

"Somebody'd better get down there fast," said Ilona.

Phil Slater waited for Follette in a bar on West 23rd Street between 9th and 10th avenues. He sipped a large ginger ale on the rocks with a piece of squeezed lime and stared at the television screen.

But his mind was not on the televised image. His mind was on Dr. Deirdre Quinn Nightingale. Was she a genius or a nut job?

The bankbook had been a spectacular find. And if it turned out to be legit, then this was an open-and-shut case. Arden Sellers wanted that $106,000. It was being held in trust for her, but she wanted it now. Schirra didn't want to give it to her. She had paid someone to blow him away.

But Schirra had been slick. He had hidden the book. Somewhere. Maybe in the same place he hid lots of other stuff—on the cliffs. Arden was searching for it when she fell to her death. Case closed. Game over. The shooter may never be found, but what went down was evident and obvious to all but an idiot.

Slater turned away from the TV and stared gloomily at the old man at the end of the bar.

He reminded Slater of his Uncle Louis, now living in Arizona. He had the same lined face and leathery complexion, old and unyielding as the desert itself.

His thoughts went back to the lady vet. She had been right about sending that kid up to the cliffs. What if she was right about the eye-witnesses not being strangers to one another? Then it was a whole new ballgame. And a weird game at that. A game that essentially negated the bankbook scenario. Or did it?

He was rarely so confused by a case. Stupid, yes. But not confused. As for the hundred and one dipsy doodle cat hairs in this murder—churches, cemeteries, mysterious patent applications, roses, bank messengers—well, he just had to throw up his hands.

The old man who looked like Uncle Louis thought Slater was trying to signal him. "What?" he called down the bar.

Slater shook his head and turned away.

Follette came in then, stood next to Slater, and ordered a lite beer from the bartender.

"You speak to them?" Slater asked.

"All of them. Except the yokels from up-state."

"And . . . ?"

"*Nada*. They just wandered into the club. Nobody knows nobody else."

"Okay. You got a notebook with you?"

Follette gave him a dirty look but nodded.

"Take it out."

"You giving dictation now, Phil?"

"We'll do some matching . . . some cross-checking. Let's run the stuff through the computer."

Follette took out his mechanical pencil and twisted the top gingerly.

"What basic stuff are we talking about here?" he asked when the lead was advanced.

"Drivers' licenses. Voter records. Social Security. Credit cards."

"What are we looking for?"

"Who the hell knows? Any kind of match . . . coincidence . . . connection . . . anything that shows us those people could have met each other before Schirra was killed. Oh, and don't forget marriage licenses. You never know."

"I don't know where you're going with this," Follette said.

Slater grinned. "If I knew, wouldn't I be in Hollywood now consulting on network cop shows and making three mil a year?"

But that was just a barroom quip. Something

off the top of his head. Slater was trying to be funny.

What he was really thinking about was not so funny. Was it possible that this upstate animal doctor knew even more than she had told him about the case? Was it possible that something else was found on that cliff? Was it possible she had the gall to have been, in her own fashion, carrying on her own investigation of the Schirra killing?

Follette finished his beer and stared into the bottom of the glass.

"What if," he asked morosely, "they all, at one time, attended the same dance class? It won't show up on any computer check."

"Unless it was ballroom dancing," Slater retorted. "Everybody knows there's a secret code on New York State drivers' licenses identifying people who have basic ballroom dancing skills."

They couldn't get a cab, so Didi and Rose walked. It is a long walk from 34th Street at the East River to 10th Avenue at 22nd Street, in Chelsea.

It had been decided to make this a two-woman rescue mission, since Ilona had had too much to drink. But she would be waiting by the phone, she said, ready to dispense expert veterinary advice if the situation was beyond Dr. Nightingale's competence in treating felines.

"Just remember, Nightingale," Ilona had warned when Didi and Rose departed, "cows are not cats." Then she modified her statement: "I mean, cats are not cows." And she treated them to an impromptu ditty about bovines and felines.

As they walked, Rose pointed out restaurants she had eaten in when she lived in Manhattan, buildings she had worked in, blocks she remembered, apartment houses where friends had lived.

Didi listened and said nothing. She was wondering how they were going to get into the place. Was there a janitor—a super, as it was called in the city—who lived in a nearby building, who was taking care of Boots? Was the key to the club also on the ring of keys Slater had found in Arden's apartment? Would Detective Slater give her the key if he had it? Or would he say, "Call the ASPCA?" And, above all, was poor Molson okay? Cats, she knew, could survive awesome trials. They could live for a long time without food—but only if they had water.

When they reached the outer perimeter of the neighborhood called Chelsea, Rose began to gush. How the neighborhood had changed for the better! And how grim it used to be.

Boots was closed down—locked and dark. They walked into a cleaning establishment next door. The proprietor was friendly. No, he didn't know what happened to the cat. No, the janitor wasn't around now; he lived uptown and came around in the mornings. And yes, the dry cleaner was happy the damn place was shut down, though he was sorry about what happened to the owner.

"Is there any way to even look in?" Didi asked.

The proprietor, a middle-aged Filipino man, nodded. "Just go around the corner. There's an alley that runs along the back of the stores. We keep the garbage there. Watch your step."

When they entered the alley, Rose said, "I would not go in here if it wasn't still light, no matter how many cats were starving inside."

In fact, the light was fading fast. The rears of the stores were indistinguishable from one another. But they found several cartons of empty rum bottles piled in front of one of the doors. And Boots was the only drinking establishment on the block.

"It must be those four windows—two on either side of the door," Rose said. They peered in, but the windows seemed to be frosted from the inside. All they could see were distorted shapes.

"Look!"

"At what?"

"The top of that first window."

Didi stared. Yes. The frame was warped. There was a sliver of space—the window did not close to the top.

"I spent the last four years crawling on top of my barn," Rose said. "I'm an expert in wood. That thing in doable."

They quietly overturned two garbage cans. Rose found some Masonite in a pile of junk. They climbed on the garbage cans, holding each other to steady themselves. Rose inserted the thin piece of Masonite in the space and levered it upward. The window moved down, the frame splintering just a bit. They waited to see if the noise had attracted anyone. It hadn't.

"What do you see?" Didi asked.

"A urinal. It's the men's room."

They pushed the window all the way down and climbed in. It was difficult, but once inside there was clear sailing.

"Don't turn on any lights, Rose."

They walked out of the men's room and found themselves immediately in the performance space where Carl Schirra had been murdered.

"I don't see your four-legged friend," Rose whispered.

Didi began to call out to the cat. Over and over she called his name. But there was no response. Not a sound. Not a movement from the shadows.

She and Rose walked to the bar area. They searched behind the bar. Then they entered Schirra's office. It was small and tidy and nearly empty—only a desk, two chairs, and a few bookshelves.

Didi continued to call Molson, while Rose peered beneath the desk.

"I smell something funny," said Didi.

Rose sniffed the air. "Paint," she pronounced.

The inside of Boots was growing darker and darker as daylight receded.

Didi spotted three small spray-paint cans on one of the shelves standing side by side, like soldiers. One of them was dripping blue paint. "Maybe," she said, "that's what poor Molson was recovering from. Some cats are very allergic to paint whether it's lead-based or not."

"What about the kitchen . . . with all those good mice cavorting about."

"This place didn't serve food," Didi informed her.

But they looked anyway. Rose switched on the lights. It was a real restaurant-type kitchen with a huge professional range, vats, basins, bins, a riot of stainless steel and aluminum. But all unused.

And there was no sign of mice. Or Molson.

"No windows here," Rose said. Then she looked over at the far wall. "What's that? That door."

"A meat freezer," Didi explained. "This place may have once been a steak house or something."

Rose walked over and pulled the large door open. It was dark. She pulled an overhead string. Four fluorescent overheads lit up. The meat locker was empty.

Except for one strange object.

"Look at this," Rose said. Didi walked inside the meat freezer and approached. It was a large enclosed box, about six feet high, nine feet wide, and three feet deep. Three of the sides were glass. The back was some kind of metal.

"What the hell is it?" Rose queried.

"It looks like a florist's greenhouse," Didi remarked.

"Of course! I've seen them a thousand times. In retail florists. It just looks strange in this setting. They're climate-controlled little greenhouses. The florist keep orchids and roses in it."

Didi held up her hand.

"What's the matter?" asked Rose.

"Nothing," she said quietly. She began to open and close the sliding glass greenhouse doors. She looked glassy-eyed. She looked for a moment as though she were in pain.

"What are you staring at, Didi?"

"Nothing."

Rose walked out of the freezer and started opening and closing the doors of the kitchen cabinets.

Didi hadn't moved. She had been looking

for an abandoned cat. She hadn't found him. But, she realized, she might have found the rationale for murder. Right here in the meat freezer within which was this strange little free-standing, climate-controlled box.

It was empty now, but it had not always been so.

Her hands felt numb, although the meat freezer was room temperature.

"Let's get out of here," Rose said. "Your kitty has vanished. I bet the super took the beast home with him."

Rose headed for the open window in the men's room.

"I'll be right there," Didi said. She slipped quickly into Schirra's office, took one of the small cans of blue paint off the shelf, and stuffed it into her back pocket.

It was easier and faster climbing out than climbing in.

Once outside, they pulled the window up as far as it would go given the warped frame, removed the garbage cans from beneath the window, and walked quickly out of the now pitch-dark alley.

"Where now?" Rose asked.

"I think you'd better get to Ilona. I'll be

there later. I want to get some gifts for my elves." It was more than a lie. It was a damn lie.

Rose got a cab quickly. Didi stood alone on 10th Avenue. Like a pilgrim in the wicked city. She remembered she had once heard a piece of music called "Slaughter on 10th Avenue."

She began to walk, then realized she didn't know which direction she was walking in, or in fact, where she wanted to go.

It was all very sad—and funny and pathetic and dangerous—but she was like a terrier who had fastened on something in the burrow and didn't know what it was, but that terrier was going to pull it out.

She went into her wallet and furiously began to search. Yes. She had it with her—that application for trademark that Trent Tucker had faxed her.

Didi had a sudden desire to wave it wildly on the street, like a bird dog leaping ecstatically ahead upon the command to flush. Her images, for some reason, were all canine—terriers and setters and bulldogs.

She had the feeling that if she was smart and brave, yes, above all, brave, like a setter going into a thicket, she could flush a killer out. Maybe a whole covey of killers.

It was hot that August night. The heat dampened her soaring enthusiasm quickly. Why be optimistic? All she had was an enormous, fertile, fibrillating hunch that had sprung full blown out of her head after somehow connecting that can of blue spray paint, the strange greenhouse in the meat locker, and the words *Hudson Blue* on the trademark application form.

Maybe she wouldn't flush out any killers at all. But she sure was going to flush someone out who knew something.

She walked to a stationery supply store on Sixth Avenue and made three Xeroxes of the application. She purchased a ballpoint pen and three manila envelopes.

Then she walked across the street to a bagel shop. She ordered a bagel she had never even heard of before—something called an "Everything." And she had the man behind the counter lather it with scallion cream cheese. Desperate dishes for desperate people.

She ate it slowly and fastidiously, with a grape juice. When she finished, she cleaned the top of the table with a napkin.

She used her new ballpoint pen to write a name on each of the three manila envelopes:

Darryl Yates
Dr. Ron Besser
Mazzini

On each of the Xeroxed applications, beneath the scribbled words *Hudson Blue,* she wrote:

I will be silent for a price.
Same time. Same place.

They would know what "same time, same place" meant, she thought grimly. Tomorrow evening at 7 P.M. at Boots.

Then she sprayed a dab of the blue paint on each Xerox.

She went to the pay phone and called Slater. He wasn't there. She gave the machine the pay phone number. "Urgent," she claimed.

Slater called back in thirty minutes. "Now what?" he asked as soon as she picked up.

"Did you find a connection between the witnesses?"

"We're working that one."

"Good. I need a favor."

"I work for the NYPD. Not the Salvation Army."

"It's a very small favor."

"What?"

"I want the addresses of the eyewitnesses."

"What for?"

She had the lie all prepared. It was a rather elegant one, she thought. "Well, I'm going back to Hillsbrook shortly. And I just want to give them my address . . . let them know if they're ever upstate . . . they'll be welcome."

There was a long pause. "I don't believe a word of what you just told me."

She couldn't help giggling. "Not a single word?"

He laughed, too. "Not a syllable. But hold on just a minute."

She rushed to her table, picked up the envelopes, and returned to the phone.

"You there?"

"I'm here."

As he gave her the addresses, she wrote them beneath the appropriate names on the envelopes.

Besser lived on West 55th Street in Manhattan. Yates on Mercer Street, also in Manhattan.

The Mazzini sisters on Ocean Parkway, in Brooklyn.

"Whatever you're doing, I don't like it," Slater said.

"And you'll be welcome in my home as well, Detective Slater, if you ever get upstate again."

He guffawed and hung up. Didi quickly slid a Xerox of the annotated application into each envelope and left the shop. She walked until she found a compatible ATM and took out the remaining cash in her checking account, $640.

She walked on until she came to an electronics and camera store that was still open. She purchased a Polaroid with a flash and had it gift wrapped to cover her story that she had gone shopping for her elves.

Then she hailed a cab. It pulled over to the curb. She did not get in. She told the driver that she wanted to make three stops—two in Manhattan and one in Brooklyn. And at each stop she wanted him to get out and deliver a package to the doorman or just leave it under the lobby door. She would pay, she said, ten dollars per delivery, in addition to the meter charge and a twenty dollar tip over that.

The cabbie said, "Get a bike messenger," and

drove off. He didn't know how macabre his suggestion was.

The second driver to whom she made the proposal looked at her as if she were insane and zoomed off before she could finish the last part of her story.

The third prospect, a portly Egyptian, accepted.

"You're late," said an irate Brixton. "I thought you said the procedure goes from dusk to dawn."

Charlie Gravis replied, "Actually, we build up to that. We always start a bit later at first, then slowly increase the length of the procedure."

Charlie couldn't tell his new client that the reason he was late was that Ike Badian's old car had balked at being worked in the brutal August heat.

Charlie and the dairy farmer stood in the center of the barn, beside the hay bales. The pigs were noisy. The cows were silent.

Ike Badian had driven off. He would return at dawn, he promised, and he wished Charlie luck.

The dim overhead night lights in the barn

had already been switched on, even though there was some daylight left.

Why is this man carrying on so? Charlie thought. It's still dusk—after a fashion.

Then he carefully removed the tape recorder from the satchel and placed it on a hay bale. He unraveled the cord, ran it to the wall, and plugged it into a socket.

Brixton looked on with both interest and skepticism.

"I was expecting a more elaborate setup," Brixton said. "You know. A real fancy machine with speakers and all kinds of precision knobs."

"Believe me, we know what we're doing," Charlie assured him.

"And what? You just play this . . . music . . . all night?"

"Right, right. But it's a lot more complicated than that. The volume is scientifically modulated as the night wears on. According to the sleep cycles of the cows."

Charlie had gotten all this language from the old articles he had read. It didn't make much sense to him, but it sure sounded impressive.

"How the hell do you know their sleep cycles?" Brixton asked. "I don't even know them."

Charlie didn't respond. He checked the tape.

"What kind of music you going to play for them? Beach Boys?"

"Oh no. A piece that has proven successful in increasing yield," said Charlie.

The ruminating cows were watching them, their ears slightly forward, tails swishing ever so slowly.

Brixton said with a sigh, "Well, strike up the band, I guess."

Charlie did not appreciate this kind of humor. He took out an official-looking notebook and several lead pencils. These were merely props, to give Brixton more confidence in the scientific genealogy of the procedure. Scientists always had their notebooks handy.

A female voice from inside the house was heard: "Roy!"

That must be his wife, Charlie thought. Good. He'd just as soon not have Brixton looking over his shoulder constantly.

"I'll stop in from time to time," the farmer said as he departed.

Charlie sat down on a neighboring bale of hay. The heat in the barn was intense. He wiped the sweat from his brow and neck with his favorite blue checked handkerchief. Then he stacked the ten cassettes one on top of the other like artillery shells. These were ten copies of Abigail's master tape on which she had recorded the song six times. This way, he wouldn't have to rewind—just pop in another duplicate.

When he started raking in the bucks, he would spring for one of those hi-tech long-playing machines, the kind he heard they used at the big radio stations—computer driven.

He turned the volume down low and pressed the PLAY button.

Abigail's voice was barely audible. He turned up the volume a bit, and her beautiful rendition of the old Negro spiritual began to waft through the barn.

That was all there was on the tapes—Abigail singing "Go Down, Moses." Six times. Each rendition a bit different, but always that wonderful "scatting" of the refrain "Let my people go."

Charlie turned the volume up a bit more. Two of the cows bellowed. Charlie was happy. He closed his eyes.

Brixton came by in about an hour, stood at

the far end of the barn, and just listened and watched. He didn't even wave. Then he walked back to the house.

The night became wearying for Charlie. He couldn't get to sleep. And there were the tapes to change. He tried for quick, intense catnaps, but to no avail. He got groggier and groggier. To offset this, he took aisle walks—down the center of the barn from one end to the other, greeting the majority cows and the minority pigs with a nod and a tip of his imaginary cap. The pigs were big breeding boars; each pen held only one.

Once or twice he walked out of the barn and stared at the darkened house and the pasture beyond. It was a lovely little farm.

At two o'clock Charlie finally got a good snooze. The endless repetitions of the song had made him dopey. He woke in twenty minutes. It was the last lap. Was it working? Probably. He had never seen such a contented bunch of dozing milk cows.

He turned up the volume another notch. He began to muse, happily. The first thing he would purchase when the money started rolling in was one of those hi-tech blenders. They cost a bundle, as much as $500, he wagered. He was always yearning for a good chocolate malted.

He turned the volume up another notch. Abigail's voice was like a soothing rain.

Through heavy eyelids he checked his watch: 3:25.

Then the mayhem hit!

It all happened so quickly.

There was a horrendous splintering noise. And another. And another.

And then a series of horrifying grunts and squeals.

Then all six breeding boars were smashing through their pens and running crazily down the aisle and out the open door of the barn.

It wasn't clear whether they simply could no longer abide the music, or whether it had roused them to revolt and they were fleeing their own Egypt.

Only four of the boars were ever recaptured.

Their freedom had been expensive. They destroyed the Brixton vegetable garden totally, including the frames in which Mrs. Brixton was growing young plants to market. By the time the rampage was over, they had caused $7,000 in other damages.

Ike Badian found Charlie sitting on the road about a half mile away from the Brixton place.

"What are you doing here, Charlie?" he asked, fear already creeping into his voice.

Gravis climbed slowly into the vehicle. "The program needs a few adjustments," he said.

Ike decided it would be impolite to probe further or indulge in I-told-you-so's. He pointed to the dashboard where a container of coffee, a glazed donut, and a small cigar were waiting for the entrepreneur.

Chapter 9

Like a surgical procedure, Didi thought as she sat in the darkness. Everything is laid out properly. Everything is ready to go. All she had to do was pick up the scalpel and make the first incision.

She was seated on the small stage at Boots, her feet dangling over the edge.

From here on in, everything was meticulously planned. She had left a trash can right under the men's room window and had not pulled the window up after she herself had entered. She knew which way the intruder would come. There was only one way. From the men's room into the performance space.

Her camera, the new Polaroid, was primed, loaded, and ready to go—flash and all.

She had practiced opening the front door of

Boots from the inside, so she could exit quickly. This was not to be a test of bravery. The moment the intruder came out of the men's room, Didi would use the camera. Then run to the front door and out.

And then to Detective Slater. Simple. Noncomplicated. And then just hand him the photograph. Tell him her vague theory. And let him take it from there.

She ruminated over whether she should disclose just how she had trapped the intruder—the threat of extortion. Money for silence. Silence over what, she still didn't know—not for sure.

Didi cupped her hand over her watch. It was three minutes past seven. Soon. The show would start soon.

She felt a bit nauseated. Was it fear or the Thai lunch she had with Rose? All day long Didi had tried to act normal. She had spent time with Ilona in the clinic, asking pertinent questions, making intelligent suggestions, pointing out the differences between large and small animal practices. She had wandered about with Rose to her old Manhattan haunts. She had not uttered a word about what was happening.

And then . . . at six in the evening . . . she had just left the apartment. More gift buying, she explained.

Her eyes were now acclimating to the dark. She found herself staring at the table where Molson had climbed boldly up on Mrs. Tunney. She shut her eyes. Oh, to be in Hillsbrook again, making her veterinary rounds in the red Jeep. She was homesick. Even the notion of Charlie Gravis's perpetual grumbling seemed accommodating.

The sound of a moving window cut through the darkness like a leper's bell. Didi shivered, grabbed the camera, and tried to ball herself up like a coiled spring . . . like a rattler about to strike.

A gentle thump.

The intruder was now on the tiled men's room floor.

Then silence.

Then the sound of the men's room door opening.

A figure entered the performance space. The figure stopped.

Now, Didi thought, it has to be now. For a moment her body did not respond to her command.

Then she jumped up, aimed the camera, the exploding flash blinding her for a moment.

She ran to the front door as planned. But a strange kind of noise stopped her as she was turning the knob. The figure was weeping—gut-wrenching cries.

Didi heard the pathetic words: "I want it to end. I want it to end."

She flicked on the light switch. It didn't work. She ran into the bar area and flicked the switch again. It worked and flooded the performance space with shafts of oblique light.

Didi stared at the weeping, babbling intruder.

It wasn't one of the eyewitnesses.

It was the murderess. But her hair was no longer long and blond.

The digital clock in Detective Phil Slater's office read 10:36 P.M. Didi sat stiffly on the chair behind his desk.

Slater came in and handed her a cold can of ginger ale and a straw. She took it, but didn't pop the lid.

He sat down on the side of the desk. "She was carrying a weapon," he said.

Didi didn't respond.

"We believe it was the same gun that killed Schirra."

Didi was silent. She noted to herself that he was now speaking in a tone different from the one he usually employed. It was a kind of official accent.

"She was going to use it on you, too. You're a lucky woman."

"She couldn't even stand straight," Didi replied. "She just fell apart."

Slater picked up a pencil and played with it. "Her name is Carol Cushmore. She used to work for Dr. Ron Besser."

"As a medical assistant?"

"No, a landscape gardener. It seems that Besser is into plants. But that was a few years back. She's been running downhill fast ever since. Her husband was a junkie. He died two years ago—o.d.'d. She had been busted twice for shoplifting in Saks. Her four-year-old boy was taken away from her about a year ago by the Children's Court. She was kicked out of her apartment six months ago . . . a formal eviction. Current residence, unknown."

"Did she admit to the Schirra murder?"

"She admitted nothing. She has said nothing. We got that data off her prints."

Didi opened the soda can, inserted the straw, and drank.

"Of course," Slater said with a bit of a threat in his voice, "you're going to tell us why she and you were in a closed-down nightclub at the same time."

"Of course," Didi echoed. "But I really think that's irrelevant now."

Slater set the pencil down. She thought she might have seen a flicker of a smile at the corner of his mouth.

"The priority now is the line-up," he said. "We called the other eyewitnesses. We sent vehicles to pick them up and bring them in now. You've already i.d.'d her. But we want it formally. You ready?"

Didi nodded and followed him out of the office into the room with the one-way glass next to the line-up room.

Follette was there, as was a police stenographer and two high-ranking uniformed officers.

Six young women marched in and stood against the yardstick wall. Didi wondered who the others were. The cops always threw in a plant or two, didn't they? Perhaps one of the women was really a police officer. The others

might be prostitutes, shoplifters, clerical workers at the station.

Each one, on order, performed the choreog-
raphy. Step forward. Turn left. Turn right. Step
back.

Slater asked Didi, "Do you see the woman
who shot Carl Schirra?"

"Yes."

"Point her out please."

"Number three."

Number three was told to step forward.

"Are you positive, Dr. Nightingale?"

"Yes."

"Have you noticed any change in her appearance?"

"Yes. At the time of the shooting she was
wearing a blond wig."

"Did you know it was a wig at the time?"

"No."

"Number three has short brown hair."

"I don't care what color or length her hair is
now. She is the one who shot Carl Schirra. I
was seated only twenty feet away from her."

Slater escorted Didi back into the office.

"The others are arriving," he said. "I'll get
back to you."

He left. Didi sat down again. Her can of ginger ale was now warm. Suddenly exhausted, she laid her head on the desk and tried to nap.

Detective Slater returned forty-five minutes later.

"Besser said he couldn't positively identify her as the shooter because the woman used to work for him. It was too confusing. Why, he asked, wouldn't I have known her that night? Maybe, maybe not. It was a hot night. He was too engrossed in the intro by Schirra, he said. He didn't even notice the bike messenger until she fired the weapon. No, he can't be sure."

He paused there, then went on in a matter-of-fact voice: "Yates said that Carol Cushmore was definitely *not* the shooter. The Mazzini sisters agreed with him."

Didi could not believe what she was hearing.

"But you have her gun!"

"Yes, we do. And we're running the tests," he replied. He looked at her in a suspicious manner. "I wish I knew what was going on."

"They're lying. They're all lying!" she shouted.

"Well, someone is," Slater said.

She stood up abruptly. "May I leave now?"

"Why not?"

"Thanks for the soda," she said acridly. Then she walked out of the precinct house and away from it as fast as she could. She walked furiously, and when she finally stopped, she realized she had walked all the way east. She was now on 2nd Avenue at 11th Street.

Didi felt better now. The shock had worn off. She could think. There was a Korean market open across the street. She went in and bought a small container of cold chocolate milk. She drank it all down inside the store, and she thought hard.

That the eyewitnesses had known one another, she had intuited.

That they had conspired together, she had not even imagined.

But now that she knew—and now that she knew the name, occupation, and emotional state of the killer—one individual loomed up in her mind's eye like some evil goblin—the sculptor who called himself Torvald.

She turned suddenly to the Asian woman behind the counter. "Do you know where I can buy a wig at this hour?"

"St. Mark's Place," she said without skipping a beat. "Buy anything there. Till one or two."

"You mean two in the morning?"

"Yes, two in the morning."

"Where is St. Mark's?"

"Few blocks that way," said the woman. And then Didi remembered that she was also only a few blocks away from that bar where she had met Tor. Her geographical situation became clearer.

She walked quickly to the strip on St. Mark's with all the retail booths selling everything from crew socks to pornographic T-shirts to nose rings. She quickly found a long, narrow booth with two racks of wigs at $39.95 each. They had red wigs, black wigs, Afro wigs, long-haired wigs.

Didi selected a June Allyson 50s-style model, paid for it, stuffed it into her back pocket, and took a cab to Greene Street. In the taxi she tried to think how a sexually hungry female would act when ringing a man's doorbell at one in the morning.

It took him a long time to buzz her into the building and an even longer time to open the door to his loft. Obviously, he had been sleeping.

Didi smiled seductively and walked past

him into the loft, brushing against him for just a moment as she passed.

She saw that he had replaced the pieces she had destroyed in her rage. She stopped at a pile of old wooden doors standing upright against the wall, waiting to be incorporated into one of his pieces. They were like orphans waiting for adoption.

"You don't seem too happy to see me," she said coquettishly. "And that I don't understand. I thought you desired me so fiercely that you lost all sense of right and wrong."

"I did want you . . . I do now . . . but . . . look . . . I was sleeping. You should have called."

"Why don't you bring me a gin and tonic?"

He went into the kitchen. Didi pulled the garish wig out of her pocket and flung it behind the stacked wooden doors. She walked deeper into the loft and sat down.

When he returned with the drink, he was more awake. "What changed your mind, Doc? I mean, that night we went out together you acted like the flying nun when I touched you. And when you called to apologize and told me you were going back home, you didn't seem too heartbroken to be saying good-bye to me either. And now—bam! Here you are. Making house calls in the middle of the night and coming on like Ellen Barkin on Spanish fly. What the hell is your story, miss?"

She looked at him defiantly. "Time is short. That's my story. And who knows if I'll ever see you again?"

"You mean you really are going home this time?"

"No, Tor. I mean you're going. To prison, that is. For a very long time."

He put the drink down, his face suddenly gone pale. "What are you talking about?"

"Do you know a woman named Carol Cushmore?"

"No."

"Really? She knows you. At least she says she does. She claims that on the night she shot the club owner Carl Schirra to death, you were waiting outside for her in a getaway car. She also claims you provided her with the blond wig she wore that night—and the murder weapon."

He didn't say a word. He looked past her. He was wearing only a pair of drawstring shorts. She could see his chest muscles moving slightly.

Didi closed in. "She said you hid the wig in your loft after the murder."

"She's lying."

"She even told the police where. Behind the stack of doors you retrieve from Dumpsters."

Didi walked over to the spot, extricated the wig, and held it high for a moment. Then she dropped it to the floor as if it were tainted. Slowly, she walked back toward him.

"Someone put that there. Someone planted it."

She shrugged. "What does it matter? This woman has implicated you. You can either go down hard or go down soft."

I am starting to sound like they must have talked on that cop show Detective Slater is so fond of, Didi thought.

Tor crumpled. He sat down on the sofa and played compulsively with the drawstring of his shorts. He began to scratch his lower leg until streaks of blood could be seen.

"I had nothing to do with the actual murder. I was not waiting in a car outside. All I did was bring her a package that contained the gun and the money and costume. I did what Krista told me to do."

"Krista."

"Yes. Krista Michaels."

"You had better start from the beginning, Tor."

He spoke in a staccato manner, like a man describing a horse race in which he had bet all his money and lost. "Krista and Carl were lovers. They broke up, but they stayed friends. They still went to their horticultural classes together at the Brooklyn Botanic Garden and the New York Horticultural Society. That's where they met the rest of them. They all became friends—Carl and Krista and Ron Besser and the Mazzini sisters.

"Then Carl bought a place upstate. He began to haunt church cemeteries up there to find old roses. Tea, musk, China roses that people planted there for their loved ones, or ones that had just been left there one morning eighty years ago and they rooted. He would make cuttings and bring them down to the club where he distributed them to his friends once a month. It was a kind of happy Johnny Appleseed ritual. Not apples, though. Roses."

"You mean at seven P.M. In the club."

"That's right. His horticultural friends showed up: Besser, the Mazzinis, and Yates."

"And the lady bartender, Arden?"

"Yeah. She was one of Carl's girlfriends. She helped him collect the cuttings."

"What about Krista?"

"Usually she sent me."

"Keep talking, Tor."

"Plant people hate the new hybrid roses," he mused. "They long for old ones. As for me, I couldn't care less."

He sipped the drink he had made for Didi. His handsome face was flushed with sweat.

"Then Carl claimed to have found a blue rose growing wild on the Hudson cliffs. People scoffed. Everybody knows it's impossible to have a blue rose. It's a genetic impossibility. You can't find it or grow it or hybridize it. There just ain't no such thing.

"But not only did Carl claim to have found one . . . he displayed it to his friends . . . in the small greenhouse in his unused meat locker. They gazed at it through glass.

"Carl claimed he was going to make a fortune from it. The trademark name would be Hudson Blue. He would grow the roses himself from wild cuttings and guard the source. But he allowed all his friends to invest. They each put in $20,000.

"But then Ron Besser took a photo of the

blue rose behind the glass at Boots. He developed and enlarged it. It turns out from a basic analysis that Carl had worked the oldest scam in the world on his friends. He bilked them out of a hundred thousand dollars. He had simply painted the rose blue.

"Krista was particularly enraged. She told the others the money could never be recovered. But she knew a lawyer who could crucify the thief. Through civil action. This lawyer is expensive, she said. But he's worth it, and it's the only kind of vengeance available to us. They all agreed. They each forked over another $5,000 for this wonder lawyer.

"Then Krista tells them that this lawyer will serve papers on Carl as he is introducing an act on stage one night. On the same night when the friends always gathered to get their cuttings.

"They all show up to watch Carl being served papers. None of them even dreams that Krista had a different kind of vengeance play in mind.

"Instead of the lawyer, she had hired Carol to shoot him dead in front of the others . . . who would be loath to even admit they knew each other after the murder. And they would keep their mouths shut in the future about anything relating to Schirra. Krista threatened to tell the police that they had contributed their money knowing full well it would be used for a hit. She sent me to Yates often, to remind him of that threat when he was losing his nerve."

He laughed bitterly. "It's Krista Michaels who should be called Gruesome, not her tortoise. She gave the orders. I did nothing but carry a package to crazy Carol."

"Tell me. What is your relationship with Krista?"

"She owns me," he said flatly. "She pays the rent, she buys the food in my stomach and the clothes on my back. She makes contacts for me, uses her influence with people in the art world. She owns my time, my energy . . . even my body . . . if you know what I mean."

"Then she told you to pick me up at the party?"

"To make contact."

"Why?"

"It seems you have a friend who's her vet, and this friend told Krista that you have a sort of reputation upstate for meddling in murders. That's what made Krista nervous."

"Did she tell you to seduce me?"

"Not in those exact words."

"And what was the price?"

"A hundred and fifty."

"She gave you a hundred and fifty thousand dollars?"

"No, a hundred and fifty dollars."

"I thought I was worth more than that," Didi said. She walked over to the wig, picked it up from the floor, shook it out, and tried it on.

She wondered what the sculptor would say if he knew she had purchased it an hour ago on St. Mark's Place for $39.95 plus 8 percent city sales tax.

Chapter 10

Allie kept twirling the beer bottle on top of the bar. He was too happy to drink. Didi was coming home tomorrow night. He missed her so badly he had begun to get crazy thoughts—like shooting off a toe a day until she agreed to come back to Hillsbrook.

Why did she always get involved in murder investigations? He was the cop. She was the vet.

He finally took a long, deep swallow from the bottle. It was good. He felt like some whiskey. He contemplated ordering a Wild Turkey straight up. Whiskey made him sick in hot weather, but he wanted something strong.

As he was contemplating, he heard: "Officer Voegler!"

Allie swung around on the bar stool to face

the salutation. He blinked. He couldn't believe what he was seeing. It was Mrs. Tunney. She was the last person he had ever expected to see in a Hillsbrook bar at ten-thirty in the evening. All he did was nod.

She said, "I am here to ask you a favor."

Allie took another long swig and placed the bottle very gently back down.

Tunney didn't like him. He knew that. He didn't like Tunney. She knew that. None of Didi's elves had any use for him, and the feeling was mutual. They thought he was trash. He thought they were spongers. And this enmity had grown ever since Didi and he had become lovers.

Now Tunney wanted a favor?

"I'm listening," he said, reluctantly.

She moved a bit closer, but not too close.

"Charlie is in trouble," she whispered.

"What kind of trouble?"

"Big trouble."

"How big?"

"A farmer in Delaware County is suing him for $7,000. And he's trying to press criminal charges against Charlie."

"For what?"

Mrs. Tunney ignored the specific question.

"If anything happens to Charlie, it's going to be terrible. For Miss Quinn and everyone."

"It sounds like he needs a good lawyer, not a cop," Allie said.

Mrs. Tunney continued with the disaster scenario.

"You don't know how close Miss Quinn and Charlie have become? He's like a grandfather to her. If they put him in jail, everything is going to come tumbling down. All that Miss Quinn has built up."

Allie shifted uneasily on the stool. He understood the code Mrs. Tunney was employing. Didi was obsessed with responsibility. To everyone and everything. A sick cow. An unhappy Abigail. A lost tourist. If something happened to Charlie Gravis while she was away, and that something could have been prevented, there would be repercussions. For everyone involved.

"And stupid Charlie brought Abigail into the mess," Mrs. Tunney added.

"Look! Why don't you just tell me what this is all about!"

She crushed her hands against her ears. "I can't talk about it! I can't listen to it anymore!

It makes me sick. Talk to Ike Badian. He was with Charlie. He knows everything."

Mrs. Tunney pulled her hands away. "Believe me, Officer Voegler, this is the last time I will ever ask you for anything." With that, she walked out.

Allie finished his beer and drove to Ike Badian's farm. The lights were out in the house, the old dairy farmer fast asleep.

He leaned on the bell until Ike responded, then waited for him to get coherent.

"I want to know what happened with Charlie in Delaware County," he said.

Ike groaned. He led the way to the kitchen table.

Ike held up both hands. "I want you to know that Charlie Gravis is no con man. He really believed those tapes would work." Then he launched into a description of the debacle. It took a full hour of rambling exposition.

When Ike was finished, Allie took out his notepad and pencil. He flipped to a clean page and began to pepper Ike with a series of specific questions. What is the farmer's full name? Any family? Where exactly is the dairy farm? How big an operation? Is it successful? What does Brixton look like? How old?

Badian answered the queries to the best of his ability. Allie thanked the old man, drove home, took a shower, and climbed into bed.

What are my options? he thought just before he fell asleep. He had none, except the carrot and the stick.

The alarm woke him at six-thirty. He bolted upright and stared at the clock. Didi would be home in fourteen hours or so. "Go fast! Go fast!" he ordered the time.

At 9 A.M. Allie walked to the bank and closed out his only account—an old-fashioned savings account. He got a cashier's check for the $3,128.55. He put the check in a white envelope, walked to his car, got behind the wheel, placed the envelope on the dashboard, and drove off.

Allie drove very slowly that morning. He was doing the right thing—that he knew. But he also knew that sometimes it requires the wrong procedures to achieve the right thing.

When he reached the Delaware County line, he slowed down even more and began to silently curse Charlie Gravis—that crazy, pathetic old man with his schemes to make a buck.

He saw what had to be the Brixton spread.

He pulled onto the shoulder of the road about fifty feet before the entrance.

It was a lovely place. The barn was crispy clean. And the house was newly painted. There was a new Ford Ranger pickup truck just off the road on the other side of the entrance to the farm.

A man walked out of the house, smoking a cigarette. That had to be Brixton. He was, as Ike Badian had said, a very big man.

The figure fieldstripped the cigarette. He's a veteran, thought Allie.

The figure walked toward the road. Then he climbed into the pickup truck and turned the engine over.

Allie gunned his motor and screeched his tires as he shot out onto the road and then careened back onto the shoulder just a foot in front of the pickup, blocking its access to the road.

He waited.

Brixton leaned out the window and shouted good-naturedly, "It's a big road, friend, and you're giving me very little room."

Allie took the envelope from the dash, pocketed it, and climbed out of the car. "Morning," he said, standing at the pickup's fender.

"Morning," Brixton replied.

"Can I talk to you for a minute?"

"Sure."

"You are Roy Brixton, aren't you?"

"I am."

"Well, it seems that a friend of mine caused you a great deal of trouble."

"Who might that be?"

"Charlie Gravis."

Brixton's eyes narrowed. He didn't respond.

"Look," Allie said, "he's going on eighty, and whatever marbles he has left are bouncing around in his head like pinballs. I know him. He meant no harm. He's no con man."

Brixton was still silent. He stared out the front window of the pickup truck. He wasn't interested in what Allie was saying.

"I know those pigs caused a lot damage and you lost a few of them, Mr. Brixton, but—"

Brixton interrupted. "You're blocking my truck, mister."

Allie handed him the envelope.

"What's this?"

"Take a look."

Brixton opened the envelope and peered inside, extracting the check. He shook his head and thrust the envelope back.

Allie didn't take it. "Look," he said, "I know it's less than half of the damages. But it's all his friends could raise. Why don't you just bury the rest of the debt. And for God's sake, man, don't press criminal charges against that old fool."

Brixton dropped the check. Allie watched it flutter to the ground. He knew what Brixton was about. He had met his like before. Brixton was the kind of man who, if he got mugged after a night of drinking, would bear little malice toward his assailant. But if you conned Brixton, if he thought you were trying to con him out of something—no matter how trivial—he would hate you to his dying day.

Allie bent down and picked up the check. "You want your pound of flesh, don't you?"

Brixton glared at him.

Allie took out his wallet and flipped it open. He held it close to Brixton's face. The farmer stared at the detective's shield and the Hillsbrook P.D. identification card.

"But let me tell you this, Mr. Brixton. If you take a pound of flesh from that old man, I'm going to get two pounds from you."

Allie handed the check back. Brixton hesitated, but took it.

Allie walked quickly back to his car, made a U-turn, and headed back toward Dutchess County.

But he had gone only two or three miles when he pulled off the road and turned the motor off. His hands were shaking. He felt nauseated.

I'm like a cop who extorts a free meal on the beat, he thought bitterly.

He wiped the sweat from his face with a handkerchief. No, he reasoned. I just paid for that meal with my life savings. But he had extorted something from Brixton: leniency for Charlie.

He leaned back and took a deep breath. He had been a cop for ten years. Sure, he had made mistakes. He had stretched the truth. He had bullied witnesses. Every cop does, sooner or later.

But this was the first time he had ever used his badge to get someone out of trouble.

Then he started to laugh, a bit crazily. But at least he had done it to save a family—the Nightingale family. A loony, scheming old man. A mean old woman. A spaced-out girl from Venus. A young beer-head who had never held a real job in his life. Yep, Didi's family. And himself, of course; the good old honest cop, so in love with the titular head of this family that he would do just about anything for her or hers.

He shifted his weight and stared at his face in the mirror. Ugly as sin, he thought.

Then he smiled and thought of Sergeant Sappington. He would never forget Sappington, his DI in marine boot camp.

Sappington had told his charges: "Ah'm a mean, ugly black marine. But you girls are goin' to learn to love me."

Sappington had crucified him. Years later, they had bumped into each other. The sergeant had bought him drinks and told Allie that he remembered him well: that he always liked kids like Voegler. Why? Because he was just born to step on booby traps. "You can't learn somethin' like that. You gotta be born with the gift."

Officer Voegler stared at the clock in the dashboard. Only eight more hours until Didi came home.

He'd better be careful. A whole lot of booby traps out there. He started the car, steered it onto the road, and accelerated through the first curve. The sudden burst of speed made him feel better. Hell, he thought, things could have been worse. Didi could have met one of the handsome, slick Soho artists she had always dreamed about—and never come back.

... he'd be caught. Too, he could think only that there were [...] Dick could push and say, "Let me [...] filled up [...] So [...] sudden and had slowly [...] aged limbs... and never gone back.

Chapter 11

They had left Manhattan at one in the afternoon for what was supposed to be a happy, leisurely ride home that would take two hours—two and a half, tops.

At six in the evening they were still miles from Hillsbrook. The first problem had occurred only twenty miles outside the city. One of the tires had gone flat.

Then they had experienced some severe dislocation with the vehicle's fuel pump.

And now the engine was spluttering. It sounded like a sick calf.

"I can't believe we're going to have more trouble," a disgusted Didi exclaimed.

"Shhh!" cautioned Rose, and then she said in a whisper, "He'll hear you, and he's sensitive."

"Who is?"

"The car. Remember, a rented car is like an orphan. Just act like nothing's the matter. It'll clear up. It's just a blip."

And Rose was right. The spluttering seemed to die down into a quiet groan.

When they reached the village limits of Hillsbrook, it was dark.

"We have now broken the reverse speed record from Manhattan to Hillsbrook by at least three hours," Didi declared.

Rose patted the dashboard. "He's slow, but he's steady," she said with affection.

As they pulled off the road into her front yard, Didi noticed something very peculiar.

"Why are all the lights out?" she wondered aloud.

"I haven't the faintest idea," said Rose as she turned off the engine.

"And where are the yard dogs?" Didi added.

Rose looked at her and shrugged.

The two of them stepped out of the car cautiously. The darkness was now intense. There was no moon. A soft, threatening breeze moved across the property.

"What should we do?" Rose asked, her voice trembly and low.

"Why are you whispering?" Didi yelled angrily. "This is my house!"

Suddenly, all the lights inside the house seemed to go on at once. The yard dogs barreled around the two women and leapt on them, and the front door opened, and all the elves trooped out.

A beaming Mrs. Tunney rushed over and kissed Didi hard on the forehead. Then she stepped back and said, "We are giving you a homecoming party."

Didi laughed with relief and joy. "But Mrs. Tunney, I really haven't been away that long. And I wasn't in India. Just New York City."

"I hope you're not angry I called them," Rose said.

Angry? Not at all. She was delighted.

Trent Tucker, standing just behind Charlie, said, "We were getting worried. You were supposed to be back hours ago."

Abigail, who stood next to Tucker, waved shyly at Didi.

Didi began to explain the delay, but before she could finish, a voice came out of the shadows on the barn side of the house.

"I guess after the New York cops ran you out of town you decided to make some trouble for us here in Hillsbrook." Allie Voegler came into view.

Didi ran to him and threw her arms around his neck. He picked her up and spun her giddily.

"Damn, I missed you, Dr. Nightingale," he said against her ear.

She realized that Rose had also called Allie. But that was fine. It was the best call her friend could possibly have made.

Allie released her. She had the wild urge to take him by the hand and run with him into the barn and make love. But all she did was kiss him lightly on the lips.

"She's giving us dirty looks," Allie whispered, pushing her away gently.

"Who?"

"Tunney."

Didi burst into laughter, took Allie by the arm, and with him headed into the house.

Mrs. Tunney had provided a big spread in the kitchen: fresh corn on the cob, berries and cream, two barbecued chickens, iced coffee.

They all dug in. Didi started on the berries and cream. As she spooned the fruit into a bowl, she covertly surveyed her elves. Mrs. Tunney was the same as ever. Charlie Gravis seemed oddly subdued. She wondered if something was bothering him. Abigail was her usual gentle, cryptic self. No one would know that her burgeoning singing career had come to a murderous halt only a few days before. As for Trent Tucker—he looked sad and lost. But that was to be expected, wasn't it? It would probably be a long time before he got over Arden Sellers.

Allie kept close to her, always making sure their bodies were touching. Rose kept saying how she had to get back to her dogs as soon as possible—but the sweet corn seemed to detain her.

Didi was pouring cream onto the berries when she saw Trent Tucker gesturing to her. He had moved almost into the hallway that separated the kitchen from the elves' bedrooms.

She disengaged herself from Allie and all that luscious cream and walked over to him.

"That lady from New York called about two hours ago," he said, as if it were some kind of secret transmission.

"Who do you mean?"

"I forget her name. The one you were staying with."

"You mean Ilona Baer."

"Yeah. She wants you to call her."

"Did she say what it was about?"

"Yeah. But it was hard to understand. Something about a sex show on television."

"*What?*"

"And something else—about Canadian ale."

Didi regarded him dubiously. Trent Tucker didn't seem to be making any sense at all. "Are you sure it was Ilona Baer?" she asked.

He nodded morosely.

Didi thanked him for the message. She walked into her small clinic office, switched on the light, shut the door, sat down behind the desk, and dialed Ilona's home number.

The answering machine said Ilona was in her office. Didi hung up and called the office number.

Ilona picked up on the first ring.

"It's about time you got back to me, Nightingale."

"We just got home a few minutes ago. The car kept breaking down."

"Well, you'll never guess who called just after you left."

"Tell me."

"That detective."

"Slater, you mean?"

"Right. Phil Slater. He thought you were still in Manhattan. Anyway, he told me to tell you that they have Krista Michaels and that sculptor in custody. And they're bringing in the witnesses to take another look at the young lady who likes shooting people. He said everyone is going belly-up. I didn't know what 'belly-up' meant. So he explained: It means spilling the beans, copping a plea. That detective has a strange vocabulary. He reminds me of that professor in vet school who used to lecture us about the varieties of *glomerulonephropathies* found in dogs and cats. Remember him?"

Didi laughed. "I sure do. Anyway, it was very nice of Detective Slater to call."

"Wait. That's not all," Ilona continued. "He told me he thought you were one smart, tough cookie. And that's an exact quote, Nightingale. Plus, he said you made Adam Flint look like Miss Marple. 'Who's Adam Flint?' I asked him. *'Naked City,'* he said. I told him I hadn't the slightest idea what he was talking about. He said that was the name of an old cop show on TV and Adam Flint was the hero. I said it sounded like a cable TV sex show. I mean . . . *Naked City!*"

She laughed again. "Slater does seem to have a thing about that show, doesn't he? But don't feel bad, Ilona. I had never heard of it either until he told me about it."

"Now comes the *pièce de résistance*, my dear."

"Oh, my God. You mean there's more?"

"Oh, yeah. He told me to tell you that the state troopers found some more items belonging to Arden Sellers up where she died. One of them was a postcard addressed to a jazz club down in the Village called Sweet Tuesdays. There was only one sentence written on the card: 'I forgot to tell you he is allergic to paint.' That was all. Slater thought it might be some kind of code and the owner of the jazz club might be involved in the mess at Boots. So he goes and questions the guy. It wasn't code. It seems Arden had taken that cat, Molson, to Sweet Tuesdays. That's where Molson is living now. She forgot to tell them at the club about the cat's allergy to paint. So she wrote a postcard—but never got the chance to mail it."

Didi was astonished to realize that there were tears in her eyes.

"Hello? . . . Nightingale, are you still there? Did you hear what I just said?"

"Yes, yes, I heard. It's wonderful news."

"Sure is. But think on this, Nightingale. I mean, from one vet to another. It was never proved that Molson was allergic to that blue paint. It was merely inferred from the case history after the patient recovered. You made the diagnosis. But you never examined him. And no tests were ever done."

Ilona Baer paused there. Didi heard her take several deep breaths.

"Maybe, Nightingale, just maybe, Molson got sick from listening to too much country-western music. Maybe he could swim in blue paint in a jazz club and he'd be just fine. Think on that, Dr. Nightingale. Love you! Keep in touch."

Ilona hung up then.

Didi walked to the wall switch, turned off the light, and went back to her desk. She sat there quietly, in the dark.

Now why am I dallying? she thought. My lover, my friend, my elves, and my berries and cream are all waiting for me in the kitchen. What am I doing here?

But still she did not get up. Her thoughts went to her mother. She realized how much she still missed her—even six years after her death. She wondered what her mother would have thought of Allie Voegler.

Then she remembered what her mother used to say when bad things happened: "It's not so bad if you learn from it."

Didi smiled in the darkness. What had she learned from her trip to the big city?

A rose is a rose is a rose—even when it's blue.

She walked back into the kitchen.

DR. NIGHTINGALE
COMES HOME

Deirdre "Didi" Quinn Nightingale needs to
solve a baffling mystery to save her struggling
veterinary practice in New York State. Bouncing her red Jeep along country roads, she is
headed for the herd of beautiful, but suddenly
very crazy, French Alpine dairy goats of a
"new money" gentleman farmer. Diagnosing
the goats' strange malady will test her investigative skills and win her a much needed
wealthy client. But the goat enigma is just a
warm-up for murder. Old Dick Obey, her
dearest friend since she opened her office, is
found dead, mutilated by wild dogs. Or so the
local police force says. Didi's look at the evidence from a vet's perspective convinces her
the killer species isn't canine but human. Now
she's snooping among the region's forgotten
farms and tiny hamlets, where a pretty sleuth
had better tread carefully on a twisted trail of
animal tracks, human lies, and passions gone
deadly. . . .

DR. NIGHTINGALE
RIDES THE ELEPHANT

Excitement is making Deirdre "Didi" Nightingale, D.V.M., feel like a child again. There'll be no sick cows today. No clinic. No rounds. She is going to the circus. But shortly after she becomes veterinarian on call for a small traveling circus, Dolly, an extremely gentle Asian elephant, goes berserk and kills a beautiful dancer before a horrified crowd. Branded a rogue, Dolly seems doomed, and in Didi's opinion it's a bum rap that shouldn't happen to a dog. Didi is certain someone tampered with the elephant and is determined to save the magnificent beast from being put down. Her investigation into the tragedy leads her to another corpse, an explosively angry tiger trainer, and a "little people" performer with a big clue. Now, in the exotic world of the Big Top, Didi is walking the high wire between danger and compassion . . . knowing that the wild things are really found in the darkness, deep in a killer's twisted mind.

DR. NIGHTINGALE
GOES TO THE DOGS

Veterinarian Deirdre "Didi" Quinn Nightingale has the birthday blues. It's her day, and it's been a disaster. First she's knee-deep in mud during a "bedside" visit to a stud pig. Then she's over her head in murder when she finds ninety-year-old Mary Hyndman shot to death at her rural upstate farm.

The discovery leaves Deirdre bone-weary and still facing Mary's last request: to deliver a donation to Alsatian House, a Hudson River monastery famous for its German shepherds. Deirdre finds the retreat filled with happy dogs, smiling monks, and peace.

This spur-of-the-moment vacation rejuvenates Deirdre's flagging strength and spirit until another murder tugs on her new leash on life. Deirdre's investigative skills tell her this death is linked to Mary's. But getting her teeth into this case may prove too tough for even a dauntless D.V.M. . . . when a killer with feral instincts brings her a hairsbreadth from death.

DR. NIGHTINGALE GOES THE DISTANCE

Intending to forget about her sick cats and ailing cows for one night, Deirdre "Didi" Quinn Nightingale, D.V.M., is all dressed up for a champagne-sipping prerace gala at a posh thoroughbred farm. She never expects death to be on the guest list while hobnobbing with the horsey set and waiting to meet the famous equine vet, Sam Hull. But when two shots ring out, two bodies lie in the stall of the year's most promising filly.

The renowned Dr. Hull is beyond help, and the filly's distraught owner offers Didi a fee and a thoroughbred all her own to find this killer. Now Deirdre is off snooping in a world of bloodlines, blood money, and bloody schemes. The odds are against this spunky vet, who may find that her heart's desire is at stake—and murder waiting at the finish line . . .

DR. NIGHTINGALE ENTERS THE BEAR CAVE

Veterinarian Deirdre "Didi" Nightingale is happily taking a break from her practice to join a research team tagging pregnant black bears in the northern Catskills. Awaiting her are the thrill of adventure, the fun of taking her friend Rose along—and murder.

No sooner do she and Rose arrive at the base camp than they run into the bullet-riddled body of the caretaker. Although local police insist the murder has nothing to do with the scientific expedition, Deirdre feels something fishy is afoot in bear country. She soon finds the paw print of a monster-size bruin, a creature that is a Catskill legend—and a growing reason to suspect one of her group is a killer. Meanwhile, the woods are lovely, dark, and deep. And, for a vet on the trail of a murderer, most deadly.

DR. NIGHTINGALE
RIDES TO HOUNDS

Taking her sow, horse, and assorted yard dogs to be blessed at Lubin's Field is one of the highlights of the Easter holidays for Deirdre Nightingale, D.V.M. Didi is looking forward to meeting many of her clients on the procession and to making new friends. But she doesn't anticipate witnessing a murder.

Didi sees John Breitland, the wealthy president of the animal welfare league, get shot dead while standing on a makeshift stage. Once the organizer of the country's biggest fox hunt, Breitland had a history of making enemies. The leading suspect is the owner of a stable Breitland shut down, but the man has an ironclad alibi. Some say the murder was destined because Lubin's Field was cursed years ago by the tragic death of a woman believed to be a witch. Didi thinks the police are barking up all the wrong trees . . . and she decides to listen to her own dogged intuitions to follow a deadly trail of men and dogs engaged in the original blood sport—a lust for revenge.

DR. NIGHTINGALE
CHASES THREE LITTLE PIGS

A lovely little milk cow is terribly sick, and looking around the rundown dairy farm, Deirdre "Didi" Nightingale, D.V.M., isn't surprised. She is, however, shocked when her favorite vet-school professor, the elderly Hiram Bechtold, warns that she is about to be questioned in a murder. A client Dr. Bechtold had sent to Didi—the rich owner of an ultramodern pig farm—was brutally slain in his Philadelphia home. The police had found an incriminating letter at the bloody scene, addressed to his lover: Didi Nightingale!

Didi hardly knew the victim, and certainly never had an affair with him. She is astounded that the interrogating cop is serious about arresting her. Why is she being framed? Didi, smelling a rat—or at least a pig—in this dirty case, must move fast before she becomes dead meat. Going after the truth means reaching whole hog into secrets, greedy motives, and perhaps some swinish passions that can get an innocent vet tried—or fried—for a crime she didn't do.

MYSTERIOUS TROUBLE

☐ **CHIP HARRISON SCORES AGAIN A Chip Harrison Mystery by Lawrence Block.** Bordentown, South Carolina is ready with a warm welcome all right—by the local sheriff. But before long, Chip charms his way into the sheriff's good graces, a job as a bouncer at the local bordello, and the arms of Lucille, the preacher's daughter. Even Chip should see he is headed for trouble with a capital T. (187970—$5.99)

☐ **CLOSING STATEMENT by Tierney McClellan.** Sassy realtor Schuyler Ridgway is being sued by a sleazy lawyer whose deal went sour, and her boss is going ballistic. Luckily, she leaves the office to show two new clients a Loiusville property but unluckily, there's a dying man on the living room rug. While calling the police, she notices that the victim is the lawyer who's suing her. His dying words will surely make her a prime suspect. (184645—$4.99)

☐ **SKELETONS IN THE CLOSET by Bill Pomidor.** It takes Dr. Calista Marley's extensive knowledge of human bones and her husband Dr. Plato Marley's expertise as a family physician to piece together the connection between a headless skeleton found in an excavation pit outside a Cleveland medical school and the brutal murder of a med school professor.

(184181—$5.50)

☐ **NO USE DYING OVER SPILLED MILK a Pennsylvania Dutch Mystery with Recipes by Tamar Myers.** Something is truly rotten when Magdalena Yoder's second cousin twice removed is found naked, floating in a tank of unpasteurized milk. Loading up the car with her free-spirited sister and her fickle cook, Magdalena heads to Farmersburg, Ohio for the funeral . . . and gallons of trouble. (188543—$5.99)

☐ **PRELUDE TO DEATH A Blaine Stewart Mystery by Sharon Zukowski.** Caught between family loyalty and the search for justice, New York P.I. Blaine Stewart finds herself in Key West risking all to clear her brother's name in the murder of an unofficial poet laureate and widow of a famous Cuban expatriate artist. As the case gets hotter, Blaine can't help wondering if all her efforts will end up a prelude to her *own* death. "Breathless, hot-blooded, edge-of-your-seat . . . a page-turner."—Edna Buchanan, author of *Suitable for Framing* (182723—$5.50)

*Prices slightly higher in Canada

Buy them at your local bookstore or use this convenient coupon for ordering.

PENGUIN USA
P.O. Box 999 — Dept. #17109
Bergenfield, New Jersey 07621

Please send me the books I have checked above.
I am enclosing $_____ (please add $2.00 to cover postage and handling). Send check or money order (no cash or C.O.D.'s) or charge by Mastercard or VISA (with a $15.00 minimum). Prices and numbers are subject to change without notice.

Card #_____ Exp. Date _____
Signature_____
Name_____
Address_____
City _____ State _____ Zip Code _____

For faster service when ordering by credit card call **1-800-253-6476**

Allow a minimum of 4-6 weeks for delivery. This offer is subject to change without notice.